PRAISE

Here are some of the over 100,000 five star reviews left for the Dead Cold Mystery series.

"Rex Stout and Michael Connelly have spawned a protege."

                                        AMAZON REVIEW

"So begins one damned fine read."

                                        AMAZON REVIEW

"Mystery that's more brain than brawn."

                                        AMAZON REVIEW

"I read so many of this genre...and ever so often I strike gold!"

                                        AMAZON REVIEW

"This book is filled with action, intrigue, espionage, and everything else lovers of a good thriller want."

                                        AMAZON REVIEW

THE BUTCHER OF WHITECHAPEL

A DEAD COLD MYSTERY

BLAKE BANNER

R
RIGHTHOUSE

Copyright © 2024 by Right House

All rights reserved.

The characters and events portrayed in this ebook are fictitious. Any similarity to real persons, living or dead, is coincidental and not intended by the author.

No part of this book may be reproduced in any form or by any electronic or mechanical means, including information storage and retrieval systems, without written permission from the author, except for the use of brief quotations in a book review.

ISBN-13: 978-1-63696-012-8

ISBN-10: 1-63696-012-X

Cover design by: Damonza

Printed in the United States of America

www.righthouse.com

www.instagram.com/righthousebooks

www.facebook.com/righthousebooks

twitter.com/righthousebooks

DEAD COLD MYSTERY SERIES

An Ace and a Pair (Book 1)
Two Bare Arms (Book 2)
Garden of the Damned (Book 3)
Let Us Prey (Book 4)
The Sins of the Father (Book 5)
Strange and Sinister Path (Book 6)
The Heart to Kill (Book 7)
Unnatural Murder (Book 8)
Fire from Heaven (Book 9)
To Kill Upon A Kiss (Book 10)
Murder Most Scottish (Book 11)
The Butcher of Whitechapel (Book 12)
Little Dead Riding Hood (Book 13)
Trick or Treat (Book 14)
Blood Into Wine (Book 15)
Jack In The Box (Book 16)
The Fall Moon (Book 17)
Blood In Babylon (Book 18)
Death In Dexter (Book 19)
Mustang Sally (Book 20)
A Christmas Killing (Book 21)
Mommy's Little Killer (Book 22)
Bleed Out (Book 23)

Dead and Buried (Book 24)
In Hot Blood (Book 25)
Fallen Angels (Book 26)
Knife Edge (Book 27)
Along Came A Spider (Book 28)
Cold Blood (Book 29)
Curtain Call (Book 30)

ONE

OUR AMERICAN AIRLINES FLIGHT WAS DUE TO DEPART from London Heathrow at five in the afternoon. We had decided to be there two hours earlier so that we could have time for a martini in the bar before boarding. That meant we had booked our taxi to the airport for two. So at one forty-five, we were in the lobby of our hotel on Piccadilly, settling our bill, while our luggage was taken out to await the cab, when my phone rang. The screen told me it was Inspector John Newman, the chief at our precinct in the Bronx.

I thumbed green and he spoke before I did.

"John, it's John. I hope you've had a great honeymoon."

"Thanks, we have. Not what we expected, but interesting[1]. We're just..."

"I imagine you're just about heading for the airport, are you...?"

"Yup. That's what we're doing. Planning to have a..."

"Here's the thing, John. How would you feel about staying on a few days?"

I blinked at Dehan, who was watching me without expres-

---

1. See *Murder Most Scottish*.

then I held up a hand to the concierge and said into the phone, "Um..."

"I realize it's short notice..."

"I just settled the bill, sir."

"I think you'll find the reservation has been extended, as a courtesy..."

I stared a moment at Dehan, then at the concierge, who was frowning at his screen. "Our reservation has been extended...?" I said, not quite sure whom I was asking.

Dehan screwed up her face and mouthed, "What?" and the concierge looked at me with raised eyebrows and nodded.

"What's this about, sir?"

"Your friend, Detective Inspector Henry Green, he's asked Scotland Yard to request you as a special consultant."

"A *consultant*? On what, sir?"

"Well, I'd better let him explain that. I think you'll find he's sent a car for you. Keep me posted, John. Enjoy your extended, um, honeymoon..."

The line went dead. Dehan gave me a "what the hell" shrug and the concierge said, "Shall I have your luggage taken back up, sir? It seems you are in the honeymoon suite for another week..." He raised an eyebrow. "Courtesy of Scotland Yard!"

"Yes, please. It seems we are."

Dehan smiled and raised both her eyebrows dangerously high toward her hairline. "Do I get a say in this?"

"Apparently not. That was the inspector. Henry has a car on the way. He will explain more fully when we see him, but it seems we are consulting for Scotland Yard, my dear Watson."

"Super."

We didn't have to wait long. Ten minutes later, a guy in his midtwenties with short, fair hair and dark glasses came in, scanning the foyer as he walked. His eyes fell on us where we were sitting and he approached, removing his glasses and smiling without his eyes. "Mr. and Mrs. Stone?"

We stood. "Are you the man from Scotland Yard?"

We shook. "Detective Inspector Green asked me to come over and fetch you. My car is outside." He glanced around. "Nice. We don't usually put people up at the Ritz."

Dehan grunted. "Yeah, it's a long story. Any idea what this is about?"

"I think DI Green had better explain that, ma'am."

New York, like all American cities, was designed on purpose by men imbued with the ideals of the Age of Reason and empirical logic, who thought, for better or worse, that it made sense to lay out the roads in a grid.

London was not designed on purpose. It grew organically over more than two thousand years, and the roads, lanes, and streets—or at least most of them—follow paths laid down first by nomadic hunter-gatherers, then by cattle herders and farmers bringing their goods to market, and after that by the increasing ebb and flow of people: drawn to the docks that send out ships and adventurers to the world's greatest empire, and receive its bounty in return; and to the narrow, cobbled streets and dark taverns of Westminster, where men plotted on how to relieve the Spanish of their ill-gotten gold, and how to squash upstart French emperors. The streets of London reflect all of that to this day.

We wound and wove and wended our way among an extraordinary mismatch of buildings that comprised the ultra-modern in glass and steel and the ultra-ancient in crooked timber and plaster and all kinds of stuff in between, including '30s functional and post-Blitz hideous. We eventually came out onto Whitechapel Road, which is long and dreary and ugly and seems to go on forever, until finally, we turned right at a large intersection into New Road. From there we made a left into Newark Street and right into Halcrow Street and stopped outside a dark blue door with a brass knob and a brass number 1 on it.

The street was just seven houses long, and most of it was taken up with the police presence: there were a couple of uniforms outside the door in reflective yellow jackets, white police tape had been deployed across the length of the house, and there were two patrol cars, an unmarked VW, a crime scene van, and an ambulance, all blocking the road.

The driver smiled at us in the mirror, without making it look like a smile, and said, "DI Green will be inside. Have a good one."

We thanked him and climbed out. A uniformed sergeant approached with curious eyes that didn't quite conceal a mixture of hostility and amusement. "Help you, sir, madam?"

I didn't hold it against him. I could imagine how the boys and girls at the 43rd would feel if a guy from Scotland Yard was shipped in to "consult" for us on one of our cases. I smiled. "I don't know. We were boarding a plane and DI Green sent for us. I have no idea what this is about." I nodded at the door. "I believe he's inside."

He nodded. "Your names, sir, madam?"

"John Stone; this is my wife, Carmen Stone."

"Detectives Stone and Dehan," he said, "of the NYPD." It wasn't a question. He raised the tape for us to pass through.

I said, "We're supposed to be on holiday."

He grinned. "Not anymore, you're not. Right at the top. Heads up: it's not pretty."

We stepped through the door into a narrow hallway. The staircase ascended the left wall, and on the right, a passage led past two doors to a small kitchen at the back. We climbed the stairs to a small landing on the top floor. There, a woman in a white, plastic suit frowned at us and said, "Who are you?"

"John and Carmen Stone. DI Green sent for us."

"Oh," she said. "The Americans. He's in there. Try not to throw up, at least not in the room. It's a crime scene."

She squeezed past us and we stood back to let her by. Henry appeared at the door and stepped out to shake our hands. "John, Carmen, let me prepare you before you come in and have a look."

I nodded. "I'd appreciate that. What's going on, Henry? We were on our way to the airport."

He nodded and sighed. "I know, and I do apologize, but it will all become clear. John, I think you could be a real help to us on this." He glanced at Dehan. "No offense intended at all. But John has seen this before. He knows all about it. Go on in and have a look, John. Be prepared. It's not pretty."

The Brits have a genius for understatement. "Not pretty" was a young woman in her midtwenties, naked, laid out with her hands nailed to the wooden floor. Her legs were spread, suggesting she had been raped; there was the handle of a kitchen knife protruding from her left fifth intercostal where she had been stabbed through the heart; and her belly had been cut open from her solar plexus to her pubic bone, postmortem. There was also a piece of paper over her face with the end of a meat skewer sticking out of it.

The crime scene guys—the Brits call them SOCO—were dusting, examining, and photographing the room. I had a quick look around. There wasn't much to see at first glance. A white IKEA sofa, a chair to match, a coffee table, and a large, flat-screen TV. She was lying between the sofa and the TV. A door beside the sofa appeared to lead to a bedroom. I approached her head and hunkered down to look at the paper. The meat skewer was stuck through it, apparently into her eye. Somebody said, "Don't touch that, please."

I looked up at Henry. He was leaning on the doorjamb. Dehan was standing next to him, frowning at the body. I said, "The eyes were perforated?"

He nodded. "Both eyes."

"Postmortem?"

"Yup."

There was writing, something printed on the paper. I knew there would be, and I had a pretty good idea of what it would say, but I had to inch around to read it. Henry said, "It says what you think it says."

I read aloud, "And them good ole boys were drinking whisky and rye . . ."

I frowned, sighed, and stood. "Who is she? Is she an American?"

"Don't know. No idea who she is."

Dehan jerked her head toward the bedroom door. "What about her ID?"

I smiled at her. "The Brits don't carry ID."

She raised her eyebrows and smiled. "No shit?"

Henry gave a small laugh. "Not since the fifties. They keep trying to force us, but we love to be awkward. So far, we have no indication of who she is. We're tracking down the landlord..."

"Who called it in?"

"Neighbor downstairs, noticed her mail and her milk hadn't been collected."

She nodded, then, after a moment, shrugged. "So what's the deal?" She looked at me. "You're asking if she's American. She has part of the chorus to 'American Pie' stuck to her eye . . . why are we here? More to the point, why is *he* here?" She pointed at me.

Henry went to answer and I said, "Let's go downstairs."

Henry nodded. "Yeah, come on, we'll go to the Blind Beggar."

Dehan winced at him. "Really?"

He glanced at the girl nailed to the floor. "Yeah, sorry. The beer's better than the White Hart. Let's go."

We followed him down the narrow stairs and out into the late August afternoon. Overhead, heavy clouds were beginning to gather. He pointed to the unmarked VW and we climbed in, slammed the doors, and headed at speed down Sidney Street, back toward Whitechapel Road.

"You probably don't notice it," he said as he drove. "You haven't been here for what, fifteen years? The capital is changing. Everybody's leaving." I looked out the window. It seemed to me that London's eight million inhabitants were all out at the same time.

Dehan spoke from the back seat. "Are you sure about that?"

He laughed as he pulled up at the lights. "There are far fewer Europeans, and fewer refugees too. They're leaving in droves because of Brexit. And a lot of the Muslim population, they're worried that a far-right government, hostile to Muslims, might come to power. They are seeing France and Germany as more welcoming, and Spain."

The lights changed and we crossed over and parked beside an old redbrick Victorian pub with white stone embellishings, tall chimney stacks, and elaborate scrolls around the date 1894 right at the top.

The door rattled and clanged as we pushed inside. The public bar was almost empty. The walls were paneled in dark wood; there was an open fireplace, a long, highly polished bar with rows of big, wooden beer pumps, and a ginger cat sitting beside them, licking its paws.

We found a table and Henry went to the bar to get three pints of bitter. While he was gone, Dehan gave me a once-over and said, "If this were something normal, you would have told me about it by now. Why the big mystery?"

I took a deep breath and let it out slow through puffed cheeks. "It's what you've been asking me about since we got here, and what I have been avoiding talking about. Not . . ." I looked her in the eye. "Not because I don't want you to know about it, but because it is hard for me to talk about. But I guess now we are going to have to, whether I want to or not."

She frowned. "Okay . . ."

Right on cue, Henry returned with the pints and set them on the table. He glanced at us both as he did it and said, "I'm assuming, John, that you have already told Carmen about the Butcher of Whitechapel . . ."

I sucked my teeth and shook my head.

His jaw sagged a little. "Nothing at all . . . ?"

I shook my head again.

He looked at me with meaning. "*Nothing* . . . ?"

"Nothing, Henry. Nothing at all."

Dehan sighed. "Okay, guys, I think we have understood that I have been told *nothing at all* about the Butcher of Whitechapel. How about we set that right and somebody starts telling me?"

Henry picked up his glass, raised his eyebrows at me, and said, "Over to you, me old mucker."

I nodded.

"This was about fifteen, sixteen years ago, around the time I came over. There was a series of killings, all in Whitechapel. They were all young women in their early twenties, all blond, pretty, between five foot five and five-eight. There were four of them: Cindy Rogers, Amy Porter, Sally-Anne Sterling, and Kathleen Dodge. Kathleen Dodge was Canadian; the other three were American. They all worked at the Royal London Hospital, in Whitechapel."

I paused and took a pull from my pint. As I set the glass down, I went on. "Each one of them had been crucified on the floor in her own apartment. They had been stabbed in the heart with a large kitchen knife, they had each had their womb removed, without skill, and each one had had her eyes perforated postmortem. All the mutilations were postmortem. Each of the women showed signs of having been raped, but presumably he used a condom, because there was no trace of semen. And, each one had a note stabbed into her left eye with a meat skewer, with that same line from 'American Pie.'"

Henry was staring at me. I avoided his eye.

Dehan said, "I'm guessing you didn't catch him."

I nodded again. "The guys who were in charge of this end of the exchange program figured we have a lot more serial killers in the States than they have over here, which is true, and so they thought I should be on the task force. So Henry and I worked it together. We had a suspect..."

I hesitated, staring at Henry. He shook his head. "John was never convinced. It was an American chap, Brad Johnson. He was one of those white supremacy militia types. We have them over here too, but we haven't got any Rocky Mountains where we can lose them and let them play Rambo. God alone knows what he was doing over here, but we'd been keeping an eye on him because he was hooking up with a few radical far-right groups, and we were worried about possible terrorist attacks."

I took over. "It turned out he knew Sally-Anne Sterling. They had met on a dating site. Apparently, after the first date, she didn't want to know, and he got mad. He sent her a few ugly messages. When we found the emails, we went and had a talk with him. He mouthed off a lot, he was an ugly customer, but I never liked him for the murders. Henry and the rest of the team disagreed. The evidence was inconclusive. In fact, there *was* no forensic evidence —or very little..."

Henry said, "We found Johnson's prints at the scene, and traces of his DNA on her bedsheets..."

I nodded. "The forensics connected him to her, but we already knew that they were connected. What it didn't do was connect him to the *crime*, or to the other girls. He could conceivably have known them—he had no alibi for the nights of the other three killings, he was in London at the time, and he lived in the area. But none of that was enough, it was just ifs and maybes. He lawyered up, got a solicitor and a barrister, and shortly after the last killing, he returned to the U.S. After that, the killings stopped, and I returned to New York."

Henry was staring hard at me. After a moment, he grunted and said, "But he's back now."

I frowned at him. "Are you serious?"

"Deadly. We've been keeping an eye on him, but as of today I'm going to request a twenty-four-hour-a-day watch. He's been here for just over three months, promoting some business he's in or something. You were deeply invested in that case, John. You had a real feel for it."

I sighed and shook my head. "We are not going to agree, Henry. I still don't believe he's our man."

"I don't care, you are the man for this job, and I would really appreciate your help."

I hesitated. "I need to think it over."

He stared me in the eye but pointed at Dehan. "And John,

you need to discuss it with your wife. And I mean *everything*!" He drained his glass and stood. "I'm going to go and attend to a few things. I will see you back here in about three-quarters of an hour. Meanwhile, you 'fess up, me old mate."

He walked out into the leaden, gray light of the late afternoon. I could feel Dehan staring at me, but I couldn't meet her eye. Finally, she said, "What the hell is going on, Stone?"

I looked her in the eye. "I think Brad Johnson killed my wife."

TWO

She stared at me for a long time while I stared at the large glass of dark beer on the table in front of me. Eventually, she said, "Your wife?"

I nodded, still without meeting her eye. "We were only married a very short time." I finally looked up at her. "I'm sorry. I should have told you a long time ago." She frowned, and I kept talking, trying to preempt her anger and disappointment. "There always seemed to be something else to talk about, or it was inappropriate, or it would have spoiled the mood. It's not exactly something you bring up on a honeymoon. There never seemed to be a right moment." I sighed. "Like I said, Carmen, it's not that I didn't want to tell you. I guess I've just grown used to avoiding it, not thinking about it . . . I'm sorry."

She was still frowning. "Hey."

I looked into her eyes. They were serious.

"You're my guy. Stop apologizing. I told you once, whatever it was you were not talking about, I'd hear it when you were ready. You don't need to apologize to me for anything, Stone."

She held out her fist. I smiled and punched it gently. "You're one of a kind, kiddo. I should marry you."

"So, do you still love her?"

I shrugged. "I love her memory. I always will. She was a very special person, and we were good. But it was fifteen years ago. I have laid her to rest." I shook my head. "It's not the same . . ." I gestured at her and then at me. "I'm a different person now. What we have is not like anything . . ."

She gave me a smug smile. When she spoke, her voice was quiet. "I know what we've got, Stone. You don't need to explain." Then she became serious. "But if we're going to do this, investigate this murder, you'll need to tell me what happened. You'll also have to tell me, honestly, if you *can* do it. We don't have to do this. We can go home."

I thought about it. Eventually, I gave a single nod. "Yeah, knowing you're there."

"Always."

"I met Hattie . . ." I stopped.

Dehan had given a little start. She smiled and shook her head. "It's stupid, but, realizing she had a name . . ."

"Yeah, Henrietta: Hattie. We met soon after I moved out here. We took it slow. I guess we were cautious about my job, and the fact that I lived on another continent. Plus, I was only supposed to be here six months." I paused and gave a small laugh. "We're supposed to be checking in and ordering martinis at Heathrow Airport. Instead we're here, doing this . . . You sure you're okay? It's the past. It's fifteen years ago . . ."

"Stone. Look at me . . ."

I realized I had been talking to the ceiling and sat forward to face her.

"Sometimes, when we don't confront something that we need to confront, life kicks us in the ass and *makes* us confront it."

I smiled. "Is that in the Torah?"

She nodded. "Yeah, in those very words. Exactly like that. It also says, 'Now cowboy up.'"

I sighed noisily. "After I got my first six months extended, I guess we both decided it was time to get a bit more serious and look at options. I could move here. I like England, the guys at the

Yard were getting used to me. We had a good working relationship. Henry was a friend . . ." I spread my hands. "Or, she could move back to the States with me. She wasn't crazy about that option. She was a talented artist and illustrator. She was known here, her publisher was here in London . . ."

I stopped and took a long pull on my drink.

She waited a moment, then said, "So by your seventh month here, you were beginning to get serious."

I nodded.

"You always were rash and impetuous, even back then . . . ?"

I gave her a lopsided grin. "I guess I was. So we started talking about marriage. We got engaged and I asked for a second extension, got told yes, but that was the last: either I came home or I stayed in London. We decided, whatever we did, whether we stayed in London or moved to New York, we would have to be married. So, that was what we did. I don't think her family were thrilled. A New York cop from the Bronx wasn't exactly what they had in mind for their daughter, but they accepted me."

"Was she from a nice family?"

I nodded. "What they call posh." I smiled. "Port Out, Starboard Home. That's where the first-class cabins were."

She laughed.

I went on. "She was posh, yeah. Her parents had a house in the country and another in Chelsea. We used to visit them, and with time, they grew to like me, more or less. I don't think they ever forgave me for not having a huge wedding, but Hattie told them she had better things to spend her money on, and bought me the Jag. She knew I would love it, and it was a subtle way of making it that much more difficult to go back to the States."

I fell silent. Dehan stood and went to the bar. She came back a couple of minutes later with two more pints and set one of them in front of me. It struck me that she could not have been more different from Hattie. But then, I was no longer *that* John Stone. She took a pull, smacked her lips, sighed, and smiled.

"So, meantime, almost a year has gone by. What's happening at work?"

"That was more than a year. That was about fifteen months, by the time we got married. Meantime, the killer they were now calling the Butcher of Whitechapel was turning into a real nightmare. He had killed his fourth victim, just about everybody on the task force was convinced Johnson was our man, but I didn't buy it. I don't know what it was. Maybe it was a cultural thing. They were locked into the idea that they were 'American murders.' The victims were American, serial killers are pretty rare here but common in the States, the first victim had had a relationship with an American who just reeked of killer..."

"But you didn't like him for it."

I shook my head. "No, because I knew he was more than capable of revenge killing, or killing some guy in a brawl in a bar, or shooting some guy in a heist. But he wasn't going to stick around to perform rituals. Johnson is just a primitive, brutish, bad man. The guy who killed these girls is a paranoid schizophrenic. Johnson, in his simple, animal way, is perfectly sane."

"So what happened?"

"There was a lot of frustration. There was no forensic evidence to move the investigation forward. We had no way of tying Johnson to any of the actual crimes. We pulled him in a few times, and each time, they either had me present at the interview or, the last couple of times, they had me interrogate him. By then, he was claiming police harassment and that we were out to frame him."

I took another pull and leaned back in my seat. "What made it more complicated was that Johnson was obviously involved in *something*. You could see that a mile away. I figured he was running small arms for radical, far-right groups over here. So that made him look guilty." I spread my hands. "Because he was. He was guilty, but he was guilty of something else."

"Did you ever prove anything, find out what he was into?"

I stared over at the cold, empty fireplace and after a while gave my head a slow shake. "No. We'd been married just a few weeks. It was about a week after I had interviewed Johnson the last time. I got home to our apartment and . . ." I had to stop. I steadied my breathing and shrugged, then shook my head. When I spoke, it came out as almost a whisper. "She'd been murdered while I was at work. In our bedroom."

We were silent for a long time. Dehan didn't speak, she just watched me. I waited for the images to subside, tried to see them in my mind as old, black-and-white photographs in an old newspaper, something that had been reported a long time ago, in another life.

I breathed slowly and steadily, and eventually I was able to talk again. "Again, there was no forensic evidence, but somebody had written on the mirror, in her blood, the words, 'back off.'"

She reached across and took my hand. "Stone, I am so sorry. I don't know what to say, what I can do . . ."

I smiled. "There is nothing anybody can do. You did it already. You married me and gave me a new life." I spread my hands, trying to stay cool and hold it together. "I went back to the States. I took the Burgundy Bruiser with me. After a couple of weeks, I went to pieces. I took three months, saw a therapist, who helped. Then I went back to work, with the determination that I would be the best cop I could be." I paused and thought a moment. "And I always had this conviction that it's not enough just to punish somebody. You have to punish them for what they have done, and they have to know that. Otherwise it is not justice, it's just revenge."

She made a face and nodded. "I get that." Then she leaned back and studied me for a moment. "Okay, so if you don't want to do this, we tell Henry and the inspector we are sorry, but it just ain't going to happen, and we go home."

"No. I do. It's . . ." I gave a one-sided shrug. "In some weird way, it's timely. It will be good to tie this up and resolve it." I gave her a smile, and couldn't keep from it fifteen years of weariness, of exhaustion from living with that nightmare ever present. "In obedience to the Torah, according to Carmen Dehan."

She smiled with rare and genuine tenderness in her huge, brown eyes. "Asshole," she said.

"You know it's mutual."

She leaned forward, with her elbows on her knees. "It's a hell of a coincidence."

"That the feeling is mutual? Not really. We are both assholes. The whole precinct knows it and agrees."

"Shut up, Stone. The fact that the girl has been killed, in the same way, and that Johnson is back in the country."

I screwed up my face and shrugged one shoulder. "It's only a coincidence if it's a coincidence, and then . . ." I nodded. "It would be *one hell* of a coincidence."

She gestured at me with an open hand. "This is either a sign that you are, truly, brilliant, or that you have been drinking too much English beer."

"I mean, if it were a coincidence, it would be one hell of a coincidence. But what if it's not? Because, you know, it probably isn't."

"That is kind of my point, Stone."

"No, I know, but think about it. Assume, for the sake of the argument, that it is not a coincidence, but also that I am right and Johnson is not our man. Where does that leave us . . . ?"

She thought about it, frowning hard. "A frame-up?"

"That's one possibility. Dehan, did you look at the note that was pinned to her eye?"

She shook her head. "I didn't know what was going on yet, and I didn't think I was invited to the party."

"Get Henry to show you. I want to know what you think. The other thing is, how tall would you say the victim was?"

She thought about it a minute. "Five two?"

"Yeah, that's what I thought."

"Shorter than the other four. Not a lot to go on."

I nodded. "I agree. Brad Johnson lives in Arizona. In a place called Three Points, west of Tucson."

"How do you know that?"

"Because I have kept a file on him for the last fifteen years, well ... fourteen years, in fact. After I got back, I contacted Tucson PD and the sheriff of Pima County, went to see him, the sheriff, and told him the story. I told him that Scotland Yard suspected Johnson of being a serial killer, but that I thought they were wrong. I did, however, suspect him of gunrunning, and of having killed my wife. He was sympathetic, and grateful for the heads-up. He agreed to keep me in the loop if anything happened."

"And?"

"Nothing happened. So either he'd just stopped killing or he was the wrong man, as I had always suspected."

She picked up her beer and sat holding it, staring out the window at the heavy, gray light outside. Finally, she gave a small frown and said, "Or he was killing away from home."

I made a doubtful face. "Not his MO here."

She made a doubtful face to match mine, then asked, "What about the gunrunning?"

I gave a small laugh. "In Arizona, any person twenty-one years of age or older, who is not prohibited possessor, may carry a weapon, openly or concealed, without the need for a license. Arizona is one and a quarter times the size of the U.K., and has slightly less than the population of London. So, if he is buying guns in Arizona and shipping them to the U.K. on a fairly small scale, that would be hard to detect. When it comes to gunrunning, if your name is Ali, or Mustafa, and you have a big, black beard, you're probably on the radar. If you're white and blond and your name is Brad Johnson, you're probably not a member of Al-Qaeda, so nobody cares."

"So you have no hard evidence that he is or was selling guns to the U.K. far right."

"No. It was just a hunch. A strong hunch, but a hunch. He was doing something, that I am sure of. But that isn't the point."

She nodded. "I know. The point is that for fifteen years, there hasn't been another killing like those four, not near where Johnson was or here."

"Yeah, until now." I hesitated. "And the killing is similar, but it's not identical."

"Because the victim was a couple of inches shorter than the previous victims? That's pretty thin, Stone."

I sighed. "It's not just that. There are other things. Where has he been for the last fifteen years? Why has he suddenly come back, *at the same time as Johnson*? That is weird. Too weird. It's what I said to you, if you accept that it is *not* a coincidence, but also that Johnson is not the guy, where does that leave you?"

"So, hang on, hang on there a moment. What are you saying? I'm getting two things from you. You're saying you don't think Johnson did it, you never did; but you're going further. You're also saying you don't think the original killer, from fifteen years ago, did it either. You think this is a copycat."

I nodded. "I don't know if it's exactly a copycat, but this was not done by the same killer."

"How can you know? How can you be so sure? The height is not enough . . . That he was inactive for fifteen years doesn't prove anything, Stone. There could be any number of reasons for that. He might have been ill, in China, in some kind of remission—hell, he might have been in jail!"

I shook my head. "Because the original killer was probably an American, or at least he was really into Don McLean. And the man who killed that girl in Halcrow Street was English, and definitely not into Don McLean."

THREE

Before she could ask me any more, Henry stepped through the door and approached us on heavy feet across the bare wooden floor. His eyes flicked over my face and Dehan's and he said, "I gather we have talked it all through."

I gave a single nod and stood. "Any news on the girl's ID?"

"Not much. The landlord said her name was Katie, that's all he knows..."

Dehan got to her feet too, frowning. "What about the rental agreement? Her name must be on that."

Henry grunted. "She paid cash, no questions asked."

We followed him to the door. As we stepped out into the leaden, gray heat, I said, "What about her accent? Was she American or British?"

"I knew you'd ask that. He said she was very posh."

Dehan asked, "That means she's British? Americans can't be posh?"

Henry laughed. I shook my head. "We can have class, but to be posh, you have to be British. It's to do with how you speak. Don't even try to understand. Just accept that it's so. She was British. More specifically, English."

"Okay, so that is out of character with the previous victims, plus she was shorter."

Henry looked at her curiously, then turned to me. "How do you feel about talking to Johnson?"

"Sure. You brought him in, or do I go get him?"

"We have nothing to bring him in on, but it might be interesting to rattle his cage. From the neighbor's testimony, we've narrowed down time of death to the last twenty-four hours. The students on the ground floor, that's the first floor to you, right? They saw her standing outside yesterday morning, smoking a cigarette."

Dehan said, "So where is this son of a bitch?"

Henry smiled at her. "He's at the Olympia, at Earl's Court. He has a stand at the Dragons, Daemons, and Dungeons exhibition." He handed her two tickets and a folded, glossy leaflet. "Enjoy." He turned to me and narrowed his eyes. "You sure about this? You want me to come along?"

"Too late for that, Henry. I'm in. But I'll be honest with you. I'm surprised they agreed to your request. I'd have serious questions about my objectivity."

"Yeah, the fact that you remarried helped. And I stressed you were only a consultant. That and the fact that nobody knows the case like you do swung it." He pulled out the keys to his car. "It's not a Jag, but it'll get you from A to B. Try to stay on the right side of the road."

"You mean the left."

"That's what I said."

We watched him run across the road, dodging the traffic, then made our way to the VW Passat he'd parked opposite the entrance to the pub. I leaned on the roof as she opened the passenger door to get in. "He's right about one thing," I said.

She jerked her head at me. "What?"

"It's not a Jag."

London has one immensely long road that runs right the way through it and all the way out to Oxford. It has various names all along its length, including High Holborn, Oxford Street, Bayswater Road, and Notting Hill Gate. We followed this road most of the way, except for Oxford Street, which is only open to big red buses and black cabs, and at Notting Hill Gate, we turned down Kensington Church Street and joined Kensington High Street. The traffic was heavy, and the humid heat was oppressive. We didn't talk, except that at one point Dehan asked me, "How do you want to do this?"

I shook my head that I didn't know. Turned to look at her and shook it again. Pretty soon, we crossed the bridge over the subway and turned right onto Olympia Way. We eventually found the multistory car park, left the car on the fourth story, and made our way on foot to the main entrance of the exhibition center. On the way I had a look at the leaflet Henry had given Dehan. It said:

SATAN'S CAVE
ONLINE STORE FOR KICK-ASS MERCHANDISE
AND MORE.

They had everything from leather cigarette pouches and customized Zippo lighters to Viking drinking horns and Confederate flags emblazoned with the skull and crossbones. There was a picture of him in one corner. He had aged, but not much. His long, sandy hair was a bit thinner on top, his beard, which had been copper, was now turning gray, but aside from that, he was pretty much the same hard-ass desperado he had been fifteen years earlier. His stall was number six six six. It kind of had to be.

We stepped through the main doors and into Geek Junction. The entire hall, which is vast, was draped in black cloth, with bits of broken castle dotted here and there. Many of the larger stalls were designed like dungeon entrances or ancient taverns from Cimmeria.

We strolled down the central aisle. I glanced at Dehan's face and smiled. She didn't look at me, she just said, "What?" and before I could answer, "Did you ever play?"

"Dragons and Dungeons? No. You did, though, didn't you?"

"You kidding? I wasn't even born when it came out."

"Yeah? I wasn't born when Clue and Monopoly came out. I still played them."

"That's different."

"Confess."

"Yeah, okay, I was addicted for, like, two years."

"It's written all over your face."

"So you're smart. Who knew."

"I am struggling not to imagine you in a brass bikini."

"Try harder. Look, there it is, over there."

We were at an intersection of two aisles. Two corners down on the left, there was a large stall, part castle wall and part bearskins. Sticking up over the corner pole was a luminous cube with the number 666 on it. Dehan looked up into my face.

"You want me to go talk to him? Get him onto the subject of gun control. How hard it is to get a piece in this country . . ."

I smiled at her. "He's a white supremacist militia man. You are half Mexican and half Jewish. How do you think that's going to work out?"

She slid her eyes sideways. "I could use the Force. I trained as a Jedi too, you know?"

"I know. But this time, let's just pay him a surprise visit."

He was crouching behind a counter that was draped with black velvet and laid on top with trays of silver rings and torques, mostly bearing either skulls, dragons, or wolves. Hanging on the back wall were samurai swords, Viking swords, and battle-axes. There were also drinking horns, flagons, and various other bits of kit for anybody bent on remembering their previous incarnation as a heroic barbarian.

I leaned on the counter and spoke quietly. "I hope you're not hiding back there, Brad."

He looked up and his eyes shifted from my face to Dehan's and back again. They said he recognized me, but he asked, "Do I know you?"

I felt a slow, hot rage begin to build in my gut, but I kept my voice quiet. "Well, that's a little rude, Brad, to kill a man's wife and not remember his face. That's not polite."

He frowned at me, then began to smile. "No, not coming to me. But you know, when you do as much whoring as I do, it's hard to keep track of every bitch you fuck and kill, and who she was married to. It's a lot to remember. Was there anything else?"

I nodded. "Yeah. Where were you between the hours of ten a.m. yesterday and ten a.m. this morning?"

He burst out laughing. "You have *got* to be kidding me, man! I do *not* believe this! I don't have to answer your fuckin' questions, man!"

I nodded, "That's true. But you know what, if I talk to my buddies at the CID about all the war games you get up to out in the wilds of Arizona, and your far-right white supremacist friends here in the U.K., they might feel like asking you a few questions themselves. Do you know how long they can hold you without charge here, Brad? Fourteen days, and upon application by a police superintendent, that can be extended indefinitely."

He shook his head, narrowing his eyes at me. "You can't do this. You ain't a cop here. I heard you went back to New York."

Dehan smiled. "You know what? I think he does remember you."

"Oh, Brad remembers me. We're old buddies. We go back a long way, don't we, Brad? Brad's the man who killed my first wife. You don't get much closer than that, do you?"

Beads of sweat had started to appear on his temples. "What the hell's going on, man? I don't know what you're talking about." He looked at Dehan. "This guy is always trying to frame me. But I never done nothin' 'cept try and make an honest living. He hates me because I'm a redneck, but hell! There ain't no shame in bein' a redneck!"

I let him run down. When he'd finished, I shrugged and said, "You know what the tragic irony of this whole thing is, Brad? I always believed you were innocent. That whole task force was convinced you were guilty, but I kept telling them, serial killing was not your scene. You might kill for an honest reason, but not just for kicks."

He looked confused. "Well, that's right. I ain't never been into that weird shit."

"So where were you, Brad? Or would you rather the anti-terrorist squad ask you?"

"Oh, man!" He heaved a big sigh. "Last night? I was at home. I got stoned with some chick and watched a movie."

"How about in the afternoon?"

"I was here, setting up the stall."

"All afternoon?"

"Yeah, all afternoon! Of course all afternoon! This is my fuckin' business. It's what I live on. What do you think I was doing the day before opening at the biggest fuckin' exhibition in Europe?"

"How about in the morning?"

"At my apartment, loading up the van, where do you think? You know, you cops make me sick! You shit and the department is there to wipe your fuckin' ass. You need a car, you need a holiday, you need a doctor, you need a fuckin' shrink. The PD is there to take care of it. Me? A regular guy like me? I have to do the whole fuckin' thing myself. And believe me, it ain't easy when some fuckin' cop has decided *you killed his fuckin' wife and one way or another you are going down for it*!"

His voice had been steadily getting louder, until his face flushed red and he shouted the last words. People turned to stare, then went on their way.

The three of us were quiet for a moment, then I said, "So what you're telling me is that you have no alibi."

He nodded. "Yeah, that's what I am telling you. And you have no evidence to put me at the scene, or instead of some crazy New York bozo and his girlfriend, they'd have English cops here putting me in cuffs. So get the hell out of my face."

Dehan said, "What scene, Brad?"

He made a face that said she was stupid. "Seriously? What

scene? What, you think you caught me out? Oh, wait, you're asking me where I was yesterday just to pass the time? Or the crime was committed in a space-time vortex so there was no *actual* scene? Get real, sister!" He shook his head and said, "Now tell me not to leave town and walk outta here like you didn't just make fuckin' assholes of yourselves."

I ignored him and asked, "Who was the girl you watched the movie with?"

"I'm going to count to three, then I'm calling security. Then I'm going to call my attorney and sue your ass!"

"Yeah, I remember you had an attorney back in the day. What was his name? You still got the same guy? Nigel? Nigel Hastings?"

"One, two . . ."

I sighed. "Okay, Brad, we're going. Just one question before we do."

"What?"

"You know Don McLean's song 'Pride Parade'?"

He screwed his face up at me like I was talking word salad at him. "What?"

"Don McLean. You know who Don McLean is?"

"Yeah, I know who fuckin' Don McLean is. What I don't know is what the fuck you are talking about. You want to get the hell out of here? I'm trying to promote my business."

I raised a hand. "Bear with me, Brad. Don McLean recorded a song in 1972 called 'The Pride Parade.'"

"So what?"

"What did you think of it?"

"Nothing. I didn't think anything of it. I don't know the fucking song. 'Pride Parade'? What is he, gay? I know he married a Jewess and he has Jewish fuckin' kids! Now stop wasting my fuckin' time and get the hell out of here!"

I smiled at Dehan. "Thanks, Brad." I winked at him. "Catch you later."

We walked back down the aisle and stepped out of the exhibition hall into the heat of the late afternoon. We fell into step, walking slowly back toward the parking garage. I pulled my cell from my pocket and checked that I had recorded our last exchange. It was all there.

Dehan said, "You want to tell me what that was all about?"

I put my hands in my pockets. "Don McLean was married for thirty years to a Jewish woman, Patrisha. Both his kids were brought up Jewish."

"Okay..."

"Brad Johnson is an active white supremacist and, like most white supremacists, he is also deeply anti-Semitic and buys into the whole Rothschild, Zionist conspiracy for a one-world government theory, all that crap."

"So it makes sense that he wouldn't be all that interested in... oh, wait..."

"Exactly. The guy who killed Amy, Cindy, Sally-Anne, and Kathleen clearly has an abiding interest in Don McLean."

She frowned. "And 'Pride Parade'?"

"He understandably mistook the meaning of the title, which has nothing to do with being gay. Gay used to mean happy, pride used to mean pride, now they are both associated with homosexuality, something which Brad abhors. So he asked if Don McLean was gay. Somehow, I think that our killer would not have made that mistake. Either way, the first thing that came to his mind was *not* 'American Pie.' He may be many things, but he is not our serial killer."

"What do you want to do now?"

I gave it some thought. "We go and have a talk with Henry. Let's see what he's found out about this girl, Katie. I also need to look at the file on Hattie. I've never..." I faltered. "I've never been able to bring myself to read the file. But I think it's time, Dehan. Maybe I have a chance here to nail the bastard and lay her to rest at last."

She nodded. "Yeah, that's a good idea. We have three crimes here, Stone, six murders and three crimes. We need to keep them clear and separate in our minds."

"I know. Three crimes and only one suspect. That's no accident."

"What do you mean?" She stopped on the corner of the parking garage. "No accident how?"

I shook my head. "I don't know yet, but I can tell you it's no accident."

I thumbed my address book and called Henry.

"John, where are you?"

"We just came out of the Olympia."

"Excellent. How did it go?"

I looked at Dehan a moment. "It was interesting. We need to talk."

"Good, come over to the embankment. I'm in my office. I'll tell them to expect you downstairs and show you up."

"Henry? I'm going to need a couple of things."

"Anything. Name it."

"I need the file on Hattie's death."

He was quiet for a moment, then said, "Okay, John, but let's not get sidetracked."

"Don't worry about it. That's not going to happen."

He didn't sound convinced. "Hang on, John, not so fast. Are you sure you're up to reading that report?"

"Yes. Just please do it, Henry."

He sighed. "Okay, if you're sure."

"I am. Another thing. The note that was pinned to Katie's eye. Have you got a copy of it?"

"Yes. Of course."

"I'm going to need that, and copies of the other four from fifteen years ago. Can you do that for me?"

I could hear him making notes. "Yes, sure," he said. "Anything else?"

"Yeah, a big bottle of Bushmills."

He laughed out loud. "Same old John Stone. I'll have it all waiting for you when you get here."

"Give me twenty minutes or half an hour."

Dehan was standing with her hands in her pockets, shaking her head at her feet. She looked up, and her face was eloquent of a curious mixture of admiration and despair. "A bottle of Bushmills? Seriously? A detective inspector of Scotland Yard asks you what you need, and John Stone, with his two king-size cojones, says, a bottle of Bushmills. You are singular and unique, Sensei. They made you and they broke the mold."

I gave a small laugh and started to walk again toward the entrance of the parking garage. "It's not as outrageous as you might think, Little Grasshopper. There is, as the old cliché would have it, a method to my madness."

"You have a reason for asking Scotland Yard to provide you with a bottle of Bushmills."

I nodded. "I prefer it to Scotch. It is distilled three times, so it's smoother. And did you know that the ten-year-old single malt is matured in bourbon casks as well as oloroso sherry casks?"

She took my arm in both of hers and rested her head on my shoulder. "Nope, I didn't know that, Sensei. You are my source of useless information in shining armor."

"You are impertinent, Dehan."

"Will you punish me?"

"See?"

"With handcuffs?"

"See? Impertinent."

FOUR

We parked on Richmond Terrace, on the other side of iron gates that are only ever opened to a select few. I figured Henry hadn't been wasting his time over the last fifteen years. We were met at one of the side doors by a cop in uniform and taken up to an office on the fourth floor. It was an office with an unobstructed view of the back wall of the building next door, so I guess Henry still had a way to go.

Aside from the lack of a view, it was comfortable in an old-world sort of way, with a small fireplace that now stood cold and a large, oak desk with scars and ink stains that said it had been used over the decades, and possibly a century or two. The rest of his furniture was comfortable but nondescript.

He stood and smiled as we came in and the door closed behind us. "John, Carmen, thank you so much for your help. Do sit, please. Tea? Coffee?"

We told him no and sat at his desk in comfortable, nondescript chairs. I was still trying to figure things out. I looked around. "We have a desk which we share, in a room full of a bunch of other detectives, so we can all hear each other think. Hearing yourself think is more of a challenge. We call it the detectives' room."

He gave a single laugh that was more of a bark. "Cubicles and partitions! That is the new way, I'm afraid. It's the same here. I am privileged to have this little cubbyhole."

That was Henry and the Brits all over. They don't tell you it's none of your goddamn business. They agree with you, have a laugh, and by the time they've finished talking, you realize they've changed the subject without answering you. One thing was clear, anyhow. Whatever job he did, it entitled him to more than a cubicle and a partition. He lowered himself into his black leather swivel chair and jerked his thumb at the window. "View's not up to much, but at least I won't get shot by a sniper." Before I could ask him if that was likely to happen, he pulled over a file and a couple of A4 manila envelopes and handed them to me. Then he pulled open a drawer and took out a bottle of Bushmills and three glasses. The file was Hattie's. While he poured, I opened the envelopes. They were the scans of the notes that had been left pinned to each victim.

I borrowed a pen from the pot on his desk and wrote the date of each note in the top right margin of each scan. Then I left all five scans on my right and took the glass of Bushmills that he was handing me.

"Cheers!"

We toasted and sipped. Before he could speak, I said, "Have you any more information on Katie?"

"Not much. No match for her fingerprints or her DNA in the system. Our ME says the cause of death was the stab wound to the heart. All the mutilation was postmortem, just as in the other cases." He frowned. "Curious thing, the clothes she had in her wardrobe were all expensive, but also very good quality . . ."

Dehan gave a laugh that sounded like a gurgle. "So it wasn't expensive trash?"

He nodded. "Exactly. You'll find that people who come into money suddenly will buy indiscriminately, shopping for labels. People who have grown up with money all their lives are less impressed by labels and are more interested in quality."

I said, "Savile Row versus Armani."

"Precisely. Now the clothes we *did* find there, as I say, were very good and very expensive, some of them from bespoke tailors, but there was very little of it. That made me examine her hair and her nails..."

Dehan was nodding. "Expensive manicure and haircut."

"Yup."

"But she's shacked up in a dive in Whitechapel."

"Odd, isn't it? Now, we have a possible lead. We started looking into missing persons reports and there is a girl reported missing from her home in Chelsea, name of Katie Ellison. General description seems to fit. So I thought I'd wait for you and we could go and see her flatmate together."

Dehan looked at me. "Flatmate? Is that like a roommate?"

"Yup."

"So if her real home is this place in Chelsea, that would explain why she had so few clothes at the dive, but it begs the question, what was she doing there?"

Henry was nodding. "Precisely so. So shall we go and see if her flatmate can tell us?"

I said, "Was she English?"

"Yes."

I nodded and raised a finger, indicating he should wait. I reached across the table and took hold of the bottle of Bushmills. Henry smiled, but there was the faintest hint of irritation in his eyes. I said, "Don't worry. I haven't become an alcoholic." I put the bottle in front of Dehan and pointed to the label where it said, *Single Malt,* and beneath it, *Irish Whiskey.*

She nodded, then shook her head. "What?"

I turned the bottle and showed it to Henry, who was frowning. Then I took the scans of the messages pinned to Cindy Rogers, Sally-Anne Sterling, Kathleen Dodge, and Amy Porter and laid them out. I said, "Are they all the same?"

They both leaned forward and stared at them.

And them good ole boys were drinking whiskey and rye...

Dehan shrugged. "Yeah, why?"

Henry got to his feet, bending over them with his fists on the desk. He looked up at me. "What are you getting at, John?"

I dropped the note that was pinned to Katie on top of the others. "How about this one?"

And them good ole boys were drinking whisky and rye...

They stared at it in silence. Dehan muttered, "Holy cow..." Henry closed his eyes and sat slowly down.

I scratched my chin. "It was the first thing I noticed. The Scots, the Canadians, and the English spell whisky like that, without the *e*. We spell it the Irish way. And in Don McLean's song, 'American Pie,' it's spelled the way it's spelled in those four notes, with an *e*. Henry, I hate to be a pain in the ass, but the guy who killed Katie Ellison, if that's who she is, is English. The guy who killed the other four isn't."

He sighed, nodded slowly, then gave his head a shake. "God, you're an awkward bugger."

I put my cell on the desk. "That song is central to those murders. He pinned it to their *eyes*. You don't get much more central than that. He was telling us, back then, 'This phrase is what it's all about. This phrase is why I am killing these women.' So it's a fair bet that Don McLean means something to the killer. Do we agree on that?"

He spread his hands. "It is, as you suggest, self-evident."

"This is Brad Johnson, on the subject of Don McLean. Please remember, over the last fifteen years I have studied Brad Johnson in some depth. He is a white supremacist who believes that gays and Jews have a special place in hell."

I pressed Play.

"Okay, Brad, we're going. Just one question before we do."
"What?"
"You know Don McLean's song 'Pride Parade'?"
"What?"
"Don McLean. You know who Don McLean is?"
"Yeah, I know who fuckin' Don McLean is. What I don't know

is what the fuck you are talking about. You want to get the hell out of here? I'm trying to promote my business."

"Bear with me, Brad. Don McLean recorded a song in 1972 called 'The Pride Parade.'"

"So what?"

"What did you think of it?"

"Nothing. I didn't think anything of it. I don't know the fucking song. 'Pride Parade'? What is he, gay? I know he married a Jewess and he has Jewish fuckin' kids! Now stop wasting my fuckin' time and get the hell out of here!"

"Thanks Brad, Catch you later."

I switched it off and held up the phone. "This man is not obsessed with Don McLean or his song." I pointed at the scans. "He did not write those notes." I sat back in my chair. "He killed Hattie, but he did not kill those girls."

He took a deep breath and let it out slowly and noisily. "Let's follow the evidence and see where it leads us."

"You got my vote."

We stood. He stared at me a moment, then said, "If you're right, and I am not saying that you are, but *if* you are, it means we have three killers. Brad Johnson, who killed Hattie; an unknown killer who killed those four American girls; and Katie's killer, also unknown, who is trying to frame the original killer."

I nodded. "That is the way I see it, Henry."

"It's a nightmare. It doesn't bear thinking about."

I smiled. "But thinking about it is exactly what we are going to have to do. It has many implications. It gets complex, Henry, very complex. Listen, can you email me the original Butcher file?"

He nodded and picked up his internal phone. "Have a copy of the Butcher of Whitechapel case sent to Detective Stone's email address. Thanks." He hung up. "Right, let's go."

We stepped out of his office and in among the cubicles and partitions where the ordinary detectives worked. We crossed the large room and took the elevator down to the parking garage. As we descended, we stood in silence, each in our own thoughts.

Then, as the elevator stopped and the doors opened, Dehan said, "We need to know what details of the original crimes were given out to the press. Did you hold anything back?"

We crossed through the semi-dark toward Henry's car. The lights flashed and the beep echoed through the underground caverns. He pulled open the driver's door and stood biting his lip.

Dehan said, "Right now, we have a pool of suspects of at least eight million people, maybe more. But if there was something repeated in Katie's murder that was not public knowledge, then that narrows it right down to anyone involved in the investigation."

I leaned on the roof. "Or intimately acquainted with the killer."

She nodded, looked at me, and nodded again. As we pulled out onto the Victoria Embankment, Henry wedged his phone into a cradle on the dash and said, "Patel!"

We heard it ring over the sound system, then a voice said, "Hi, boss, 'sup?"

"I want you to look up every article that was published on the Butcher of Whitechapel. I want to know exactly what was released to the press."

"Am I looking for anything in particular?"

"Yeah . . ." He looked at Dehan in the mirror. "Consistencies between Katie and the original four that were *not* reported. Do you understand?"

There was a moment's silence. Then Patel said, "So we are saying that this is a different killer?"

"Bright boy. But, Pat? Keep this under your hat. If I find anyone has got wind of this, I'll skin you alive and feed you to my children, understood?"

"Gotcha, boss. I'm on it."

Dehan was quiet for a moment, then asked, "So, you have nice kids, huh?"

With no trace of humor, Henry replied, "Keep 'em hungry, keep 'em keen."

We made a big loop, then drove down Whitehall to Millbank, past Parliament Square and the Palace of Westminster, and followed the river Thames for twenty minutes in a steady flow of heavy traffic. Gradually, the trees and gardens became more abundant and the buildings became smaller, and soon we turned right, in among residential streets of elegant, Georgian houses with stoops and sash windows that were vaguely reminiscent of parts of New York.

Eventually, we pulled up outside a large redbrick house, with the first floor painted in brilliant white and a large rubber plant tree shading a short path to the front door. We followed Henry down that path and he rang the bell. It was opened after a moment by a young blond woman in pink shorts and bare feet, who was wearing a blue sweatshirt and a worried expression.

"Are you the police?"

He showed her his badge. "Detective Inspector Henry Green, miss, and these are Detectives Stone and Dehan from New York. They are accompanying me in this investigation. May we come in?"

"Of course." She stepped back and pointed to an invisible door. "Through there. Would you like some tea?"

She showed us through to a big, airy living room with calico sofas and armchairs, and plates, mugs, and pizza boxes on the floor. She hastily started gathering them up while fingering unbrushed hair from her face. "Grab a seat, I'll put the kettle on, sorry...!"

She left the room. I saw Dehan glance at her watch. It was six p.m., but still bright outside. We heard water gushing into a kettle, and a moment later, the blond girl came back and sat next to Dehan on the sofa. "I didn't get much sleep last night. It's a bit worrying, isn't it?"

Henry smiled like a kind uncle. "Are you Sarah Hamilton?"

"Oh, yes, sorry! Should have said. Not really myself..."

Dehan observed her through slightly narrowed eyes. "You are Katie's roommate?"

"No! Heavens no! We share the *whole house*. I'm more of a *house*mate. I mean, it's her house. Her father bought it for her. But I help to cover the bills, and the council tax is just *awful*!" She looked at Henry and muttered, "We've been friends forever."

Dehan smiled. "That's nice. Have you got a photograph of her?"

"Gosh, yes!"

I had already seen them. There were four of them on the bookcases that had been built into the alcoves on either side of the fireplace. Two were with Sarah and some guys, one was with an older man who looked like her dad, and another with an older woman I figured was her mother. It was Katie who was now lying at the morgue.

She got up and grabbed the largest of the framed photographs and handed it to Henry. He looked at it without expression and handed it to Dehan. Sarah was watching her face with anxious eyes. I should have left it to Henry, but I knew that however bad the truth is, not knowing is worse. So I said, "Sarah, I'm afraid we have bad news for you. You might want to sit down."

She went very pale and sat carefully on the sofa. Her eyes were already welling up.

"I'm afraid Katie has been killed."

Her lower lip curled in and the tears spilled from her eyes. Dehan, in that weird, paradoxical way she has, edged closer and put her arms around her. Sarah sobbed, shaking silently, with her face buried in Dehan's neck. After a moment, we heard the click of the kettle in the kitchen. Henry stood and said quietly, "I'll make some tea," and walked out on quiet feet.

I sat a moment in the large armchair, where Katie must have sat a hundred times, looking out at the quiet, leafy street, thinking about Freud's words, ". . . we are never so defenseless against suffering as when we love, never so helplessly unhappy as when we have lost our loved object, or its love." And I wondered about those people who go through life believing they have the right to destroy other people's lives and rob them of their loved ones.

Henry returned, carrying a tray with a teapot and four colorful mugs. I made room on the littered coffee table and he set it down. There followed a bizarre ritual in which he poured out the tea and asked each of us in turn if we wanted milk and sugar, and we told him which and how much of which. It had a strangely calming and sobering effect on Sarah. By the time he got to her, she had stopped convulsing and was able to wipe her eyes on her sleeve. Henry handed her a handkerchief and she blew her nose, then told him a cloud of milk and one sugar.

Tea and the British is a thing that not even they understand, but it's real. After a moment, Henry returned to his chair and sat.

"Sarah, I know this has been a terrible shock. Do you feel up to answering a few questions?"

She nodded. "I'll do my best. What happened? Was she mugged or what?"

He sighed. "That's what we're trying to understand. Did she, to the best of your knowledge, Sarah, did she have another flat somewhere?"

Her face, slightly puffy and red, registered surprise and confusion. "Only Chiddie's place. I mean her daddy's house, in Sussex."

"Can you think what she would have been doing in a flat in Whitechapel?"

"*Whitechapel?*" She actually laughed. You might as well have asked the debutante daughter of a Boston Brahmin if she had an apartment in Hunts Point in the Bronx. "Good heavens, no! Katie? Never!" She shook her head, confused. "Are you sure this isn't some ghastly mistake? Katie wasn't even *in* London. She's been away on holiday."

FIVE

I SET MY MUG DOWN CAREFULLY ON THE HEARTH BESIDE me and leaned forward with my elbows on my knees. "Where did she say she was going on holiday, Sarah?"

"Well, that's the thing." She blew her nose and mopped her eyes. "She didn't. She was very excited about it, but couldn't tell me where she was going. It was all very hush-hush and I supposed it was to do with her work."

Dehan sipped her tea. "She had a job?"

"Sort of. She was a reporter on the local paper. You know the sort of thing: Mrs. Henshaw had to call the local fire brigade to rescue her kitten, Mittens, from the sycamore at the end of her garden. Protest over awning at landmark corner shop. Sometimes she did the horoscope too, under the name Madam Stardust. She was awfully good. And of course the social pages: who was in town, who was away. She knew everyone, so that was easy for her. But what she *really* wanted to do was to be a proper reporter..."

Dehan cut her short. "So, in what way, Sarah, do you think that her holiday was connected to her job? You said it's a local paper, so why would they send her away to report on somebody else's kittens?"

She smiled and Sarah laughed. It sounded a bit like a braying donkey and was kind of infectious. Dehan started laughing too and Sarah leaned back and put her fingertips on Dehan's arm. "No! Silly! Sorry! Silly me! I should have explained. Katie's daddy is frightfully important and he has all sorts of connections, and Katie was tapping him for information she could use in a feature which she was going to offer, as a scoop, to the *Telegraph*. She was frightfully clever like that."

Dehan had stopped laughing. She looked over at me and her face said we had been here before[1].

I asked, "Who's her father?"

"Lord Chiddester."

Henry's eyebrows shot up. "Oh, *Katie Ellison*! Charles Ellison, Lord Chiddester's daughter."

Sarah gazed at him with glazed eyes. "Yes . . . sorry. I thought you realized that."

Dehan was frowning like she was getting a headache. "So is it Ellison or Chiddester?"

I said, "It's a complicated system." I looked at Sarah. "What is he, a marquis?"

"Yes, the Marquis of Chiddester."

I turned back to Dehan. "Chiddester is a place in West Sussex. Charles Ellison is the Marquess of Chiddester, so he is known as Lord Chiddester." I smiled. "His close friends probably call him Chiddester or Chiddie, though his given name is Charles and his surname is Ellison. His daughter didn't have a title yet, so she was plain Katie Ellison. If she had inherited her father's title, she would have become the Marchioness, Lady Chiddester."

She nodded for a while and Sarah started to cry quietly again. Dehan reached out and took her hand. "So Katie's dad is a marquis, and she was pumping him for information for an article —a scoop—that she was planning to sell to a major paper?"

Sarah nodded.

---

1. See *The Heart to Kill*.

I asked her, "Have you any idea what the article was about? Did she tell you anything at all about it?"

She shook her head. "No. She was very tight-lipped about it. It was a huge adventure for her. Everything was. And she loved being secretive and mysterious. It's going to be so strange without her around."

"Have you got a telephone number where we can contact Lord Chiddester?"

She reached in the pocket of her pink shorts and pulled out an iPhone. She looked through her address book and found his private cell phone. Henry made a note and so did Dehan.

While they typed, I asked her, "What about her romantic life, Sarah? Did she have a boyfriend?"

"I don't know."

I was surprised and my face told her so. She gave a small laugh. "She *had* been going out with Mark, but that was nothing serious and they just stopped seeing each other a couple of months ago. She was getting more involved in what she called 'her work' and I think they just got bored of each other..."

I could sense there was more, so I asked her, "But...?"

"Well, she had gone out on a few evenings recently, a bit more togged up than usual."

Dehan looked at me. "Togged up?"

"Dressed up, looking smart."

She nodded, then turned back to Sarah. "So you think she was meeting a guy?"

"Why else would you tog yourself up?"

Dehan shrugged and made a face. "To meet an editor?"

"It's possible, but it was rather late at night and she was definitely going for sexy rather than motivated journalist. She'd also had a few phone calls that involved a lot of muttering and giggling, and she wouldn't tell me afterwards who they were from, and when I tried to check her mobile, she was frightfully cross."

"When was the last time you heard from Katie, Sarah?"

"Day before yesterday. She telephoned to say she was coming

home. I was thrilled. I was beginning to miss her. She'd been away almost two weeks."

"Did she say exactly *when* she was coming home?"

Sarah thought for a moment. "Well, she said, 'I'll see you tomorrow,' but she didn't say what time or anything like that."

Dehan nodded like she understood and asked, "Do you mind if we have a look around in her room?"

She told us she didn't and we climbed the stairs to the bedrooms. It was clean but in the kind of mess you would expect from a young, single girl sharing a house. We found pretty much what I had expected to find, nothing. Anything of any interest would have been in the apartment. While Henry and Dehan snooped around, I stepped onto the landing, where Sarah was leaning with her back against the wall, crying silently.

I put my hand on her shoulder and she blinked tears at me. "Sorry."

"Where did she work, Sarah?"

She pointed to the end of the landing where there was a small box room with a desk and a computer. I stepped in and had a look around. There was a tall, narrow bookcase against the wall beside the desk. I scanned the titles. There were a few on journalism, mostly relating to libel and how to avoid it, but the bulk of the titles were on political philosophy, the European Union, economic liberalism, Communism, the rise of the far right, and Islam.

I turned and called, "Henry!" He poked his head out the bedroom door. I gestured with my head at the bookcase. "Have a look. I think we have some idea what the article was about." He came in and, while he was gazing at the titles, I said, "Maybe you should get your forensic IT team to have a look at the computer. Two gets you twenty there's at least one rough draft on there."

He nodded and pulled out his cell. Dehan came out of the bedroom, holding a sheet balled up in her hands. She smiled at Sarah. "Have you got a plastic bag I can put this in?"

Sarah looked a little uncertain but went downstairs to get a bag anyway. Dehan held up the sheet. "Maybe I'm wrong, but I have a feeling this is going to tell us who replaced Mark."

Henry spoke into his cell. "Yeah, DI Green here, I need a SOCO team at Oakley Gardens, in Chelsea, number seven. Correct, I also need an IT team. I'll meet them outside." He hung up and spoke to Sarah. "Do you need us to call anybody? Have you got somebody who can stay with you?"

She gave a wet smile. "It's okay, I . . ." She hesitated and looked embarrassed. "I've called Mark. He's devastated. He's coming over now."

We stepped out into the early evening. Summer evenings are long and light in England, and dusk was still a couple of hours away. Dehan trotted down the stairs two at a time and rested her ass on the hood of Henry's car as she watched us come down the stairs. Henry was shaking his head. "We'll have to muzzle the media. I don't like where this is going."

I offered him my right-handed lopsided grin and said, "It's going where the evidence takes it, remember?"

"Nothing is ever simple with you, is it, John?" He turned to Dehan. "Any other copper picks up a murder and it's jealousy, or rape, or burglary got out of hand." He jerked his thumb at me. "Get this git involved and before you know it, you have political conspiracies involved."

Dehan made a guttural noise like, "Mhmhmhm . . ." which I figured was some kind of laughter. I shrugged.

"It was never going to be jealousy or burglary. Right from the start, you had the murderer trying to frame a fifteen-year-old serial killer. That tells you straight off it was not only premeditated but very carefully planned. And smart. If that killer had four unsolved murders under his belt, the chances were good a fifth would get shelved right along with the other four."

He nodded and I went on. "You don't plan something this elaborate out of jealousy. You know that as well as I do. Most planning in that kind of killing comes after the event: How to cover it up? This kind of forward planning . . ."

He sighed and stared down at his feet. "It usually comes with a nonsexual motive, usually money: inheritance, avoiding a divorce settlement, getting rid of an awkward business partner . . ."

Dehan crossed her arms and added, "Or somebody who is trying to blackmail you. So what do you know about Lord Chiddester?"

He eased himself up onto his toes, then slowly lowered himself again while chewing his lip. "Conservative Member of Parliament for Chiddester." He glanced at Dehan. "The equivalent in the States would be a Republican congressman, but without the flat Earth religious fundamentalism."

She raised an eyebrow at him.

He hurried on. "He is somewhat to the right of the Conservatives, notorious for his anti-Islamic stance, very vocal against immigration, campaigned for Brexit, very liberal free marketeer. Very supportive of Israel. Gave up his seat in the Lords so that he could take a seat in the Commons. In the running as a future prime minister." He puffed out his cheeks and blew. "Speaking of which, I need to give him a call. Excuse me."

We watched him walk away down the sidewalk, holding the phone to his ear. After a moment, he stopped and began to talk quietly.

I looked at Dehan. "What do you make of it?"

She hugged herself with her arms and narrowed her eyes. "I want to make a big graph and draw in all the bits and try to connect them."

I nodded.

She went on, "We have a serial killer who killed four women over a period of . . . ?"

"Fourteen months."

"Fourteen months, fifteen years ago. He stops, suddenly, for no apparent reason. Fifteen years later, another murder is committed, identical to those four in every detail except one: the spelling of whiskey is anglicized. So the new killer is very familiar with the old crimes, but not familiar with the song 'American Pie,' and not familiar with how Americans spell whiskey. He is an Englishman who is very familiar with the case."

"We need to make an initial list of who those men might be."

She ignored me and carried on. "Okay, so that's one corner of our graph, up here." She indicated a large, imaginary graph in the air and pointed to it in the top left corner. "Meanwhile, down here . . ."—she indicated the middle—"we have the victim, romantically, or at least sexually, involved with a new and mysterious man."

"Or woman."

"Or woman, and highly motivated to pursue her career, or adventure, as an investigative journalist. And it looks very much as though she had identified a subject to investigate . . ." She paused and pointed at me with her finger, like a gun. "Oh, Lord! I am beginning to talk like you."

"Stay with it, Grasshopper, you're doing well."

"Her father is a right-wing politician who is very outspoken and is tipped by some as a future prime minister. We don't know what his relationship with his daughter is like, but it seems she turned to him for help in her research. Whether she got any help, and what that help was, could be important." She looked at me. "What else?"

"Just over two weeks ago, she told Sarah she was going on holiday. Did she go? We don't know, but it would seem she went instead to Whitechapel and shacked up in that small apartment. Question: Was she there the whole two weeks?" I sighed. "We need the bedding from the apartment tested and the results compared with the sheet you took from here."

Down the road, Henry hung up and started walking back toward us. He looked drawn and tired. He spoke as he walked. "He's on his way to the morgue now to identify the body. I asked if he'd mind answering a few questions, but he said it was out of the question. He had to go and inform his wife down in West Sussex, and be with her."

Dehan frowned and exploded, "Doesn't he want his daughter's killer caught?"

Henry stared at her a moment, then said, "Well, you'll have to ask him that, Carmen. He said we could go and talk to him tomorrow morning at his offices in Little College Street, opposite the Houses of Parliament, at half past ten." He frowned a moment. "Don't be too harsh on him. People deal with grief in different ways. For some people, the only way they can deal with it is to act as though it had never happened and bury their feelings. We're a bit like that over here."

Her cheeks flushed and she glanced at me. I smiled at the sight. You didn't often see Dehan embarrassed.

In that moment, an unmarked car and a police van turned into the street. Henry raised his hand to them, and the driver of the car saw us and pulled up outside Sarah's house with the van just behind him. They started climbing out and assembling their equipment, and Henry made to move toward them. I held out my hand and smiled. "Keys, Henry. You owe me a car. You want me to drive you anywhere?"

He shook his head. "I'll get a ride with the IT lads. I'll see you tomorrow morning. Ten o'clock sharp at the Yard."

He tossed me the keys and I handed them to Dehan. "You drive, I read." I showed her the file on Hattie. "See you tomorrow, Henry."

He sighed, and as I climbed in the passenger seat, I heard him say, "I have a bad feeling about this..."

I always said he was intuitive.

As we pulled away, I opened the file. I knew exactly what I was looking for and I ignored the photographs, and the description of the crime scene. I didn't want to know about any of that. Not yet. I'd been there. I'd seen it. I wanted to know if she had fought. I knew her temperament. I knew her character. I knew that she could well have fought. That she would surely have fought.

She had.

They had recovered organic material from under her nails.

They had got a DNA profile, but there had been no match on the database. I nodded and tossed the file in the back of the car. That was all I had wanted to know.

SIX

I didn't sleep that night. I lay staring at the ceiling till two. Then I pulled a chair over by the window overlooking Green Park and, by the filtered light of the streetlamps on Piccadilly, I read the file that had been haunting me for fifteen years. My worst fears about how she had died were realized. Everything I had dreaded was true. It had all happened a decade and a half in the past, but in my mind, in my emotions, it was still happening, it was still real, and it was like a fever.

At seven, Dehan awoke and swung her legs out of the bed. She sat staring at me with sleepy eyes. "Have you been there all night?"

I nodded.

She came over on long, unsteady legs and gave my head a hug. Then she went to have a shower. While she was gone, I called Henry's office, knowing he wouldn't be there. A girl's voice answered after the third ring and said, "Detective Inspector Henry Green's office."

"Good morning, this is Detective John Stone, I am consulting on the Katie Ellison case..."

"Oh yes, good morning, Detective Stone. Up bright and early! How can I help you?"

"I'm preparing for a meeting with Henry and Lord Ellison this morning. I meant to get a copy of the case file yesterday but everything was so rushed, I was wondering if you could email it to me."

"No problem. Just give me your email and I'll send it right over."

I told her, thanked her, and hung up. A minute later, the email arrived on my phone. I opened up the attachment and filed through it until I found Brad Johnson's address. 11 Raddington Road, just off the Portobello Road.

I took a sheet of the hotel notepaper and scrawled a note on it.

JUST POPPED OUT. *Back in half an hour.*
S

THEN I CALLED down and had them bring the car out front. It was seven twenty and the traffic was not heavy yet. I took Park Lane, Bayswater Road, and Ladbroke Grove, and a drive that should have taken me twenty minutes took fifteen. I turned into Portobello Road, accelerated, made the tires complain as I turned into Raddington, and skidded to a halt outside his block. It was a small apartment building with four stories, and his was the top floor.

When you've spent almost thirty years working as a cop in the Bronx, you learn something about picking locks. A Swiss Army knife and a tough heel to your hand is one of the most efficient methods I know, and I know a few. Thirty seconds and I was climbing the stairs to his apartment.

I gave his front door the same treatment: rammed the small screwdriver in the lock, hammered it hard with the heel of my hand, and turned. As I pushed open the door and walked into the narrow, dark hallway, he was stepping out of his kitchen in his shorts, holding a mug of coffee and frowning. "What the . . . ?"

I said, "Don't worry, I have a warrant."

He made a face like brain-ache and said, "Huh? Where?"

It was a stupid question. I smiled and said, "Here," and smashed the heel of my hand into his face. His mug went flying and he staggered back against the doorjamb. Before he could recover, I grabbed the back of his head with my left hand and slammed the heel of my right into his nose. Then I hit him again in the mouth, and then I couldn't stop and kept hammering at him till his face was a bloody mess. After that, I let him drop to the floor, knelt on his chest, and spoke softly to him.

"You raped, tortured, and murdered an innocent woman, the woman I loved. We were married just a few weeks and you tortured and killed her. I am not going to allow you to ruin the rest of my life, or my wife's. I am done chasing you—almost."

I'm not proud of what I did next, but I like to tell myself it was out of necessity, not revenge. Maybe I'll never know. I stood and rammed my heel hard on his right knee, breaking it. His scream is something I will never forget. There was a human part of me that felt compassion, and that is the part of me I want to say is the real me. But there was another part, a diabolical side, that was in indescribable pain, and hungry for revenge. That part found satisfaction in his scream.

I went and thoroughly washed my hands and the sink. Then I called Henry.

"Morning, John. How are you this bright day?"

"Henry, listen, I came to talk to Johnson at his apartment. I found the door open and he's been badly beaten. I think he has a broken leg. He's going to need hospitalization, can you arrange an ambulance?"

He was quiet for a long moment. When he spoke, his voice was real serious. "John, tell me you haven't . . ."

I interrupted him. "I haven't. This guy needs help, fast. We can talk about what happened afterwards."

"All right. It's on its way."

I hung up. Johnson had passed out. I went to the bathroom

and found some cotton wool. From the kitchen I got a couple of freezer bags. Then I mopped up the gore from his face, making sure I saturated each bud as thoroughly as I could with blood and mucus, and filled the two bags.

After five minutes, I heard the sirens approaching outside. I stood and left the apartment, ran down the stairs, climbed in the car, and drove away. I didn't go back to the hotel. I drove fast down Ladbroke Grove and turned left at the end into Notting Hill Gate. I parked outside the UPS store, then pushed into the WH Smith stationers a few doors down. I bought a padded manila envelope and a notepad. Then I went back to the car, put one of the bags of cotton wool into the envelope, and wrote a note:

To Inspector John Newman

Sir, I will be able to confirm later today that this blood and mucus was recovered from the man who raped, tortured, and murdered my first wife. He is an American national, resident in Arizona. I want him extradited and tried there. They have jurisdiction.

By the time you receive this I will have emailed you the results of the DNA comparison.

John

I SEALED the envelope and addressed it as private and highly confidential. Then I went in and sent it to be delivered the next morning. I knew I was playing a high-risk game, but in that moment I didn't give a damn.

I drove back to the hotel and was told by the concierge that Mrs. Stone was having breakfast in the dining room. I looked at my watch. It was a quarter to nine.

She watched me cross the large, elegant dining room with narrowed eyes. As I sat, she raised an eyebrow at me. I was rescued by a waiter who asked if I would be having breakfast. I told him I'd have black coffee and a couple croissants.

When he'd gone, Dehan said, "I can tolerate anything, put up with anything, and will forgive anything, except infidelity, which carries the death penalty, and being cut out, which carries a penalty worse than death." She paused and gave me a horrible smile. "Make me happy again while I am still joking."

I nodded a few times. "You're right. I want you to understand that what I am going to tell you, I never told you. I have never done anything like this before, and I hope I will never do anything like it again. But I don't regret it. The law is fine, Dehan, for generalities, but occasionally there is a particular, some unique situation, that the law cannot cover." I shook my head. "I am not justifying anything, Carmen. I don't care if the world approves or not. I did what I did and I would do it again, though I pray I never have to."

She waited a moment. "What did you do, Stone?"

The waiter brought my coffee and a couple of hot croissants in a basket. I took one and broke it open.

"Dehan, there is an important difference between the British legal system and our own. It's one, I think most cops would agree, where the Brits got it right. Back home, illegally obtained evidence is ruled inadmissible . . ."

She frowned at me and spoke through a mouthful of croissant. "Hereishnomph?"

"Here it is not. Here it is assessed on its probative value. If the judge deems it probative of either the prosecution or the defense's case, it is admitted."

She started to nod approval, then the meaning of my words dawned on her. She swallowed and said, "Oh my God, Stone, what have you done?"

"I read in Hattie's file that she fought her attacker. She clawed at him while he raped and tortured her. They recovered his DNA from under her fingernails and ran a profile, but there was no match in the system. So I went to his apartment this morning. His address is in the Katie Ellison file. I broke in, I beat him to a pulp, and saturated several cotton buds with his blood. I sent half of them to the inspector back home. I want him to pull strings, do whatever he has to do. Johnson has to stand trial in Arizona."

She shook her head. "You're crazy. Even if you pull it off, he won't wait to be extradited. He'll bolt. Anyway, Arizona hasn't got jurisdiction over a murder committed in the U.K."

"Wrong on both counts. U.S. courts have jurisdiction over any American who commits a crime anywhere in the world. And as for him bolting . . ." I shook my head. "He's going to be in hospital for at least a month."

Her expression was one of horror. "What the hell did you do to him, Stone?"

"I broke his leg. He won't be running anywhere."

"Stone! You could go to prison."

I shook my head. "I don't know what you're talking about. I got there, I wanted to ask him some questions about his non-alibi, and found the door open. I saw him lying in the kitchen doorway, bleeding badly. I immediately called Henry, cleaned him up a bit, and left as soon as I heard the ambulance arriving. It had slipped my mind we had a meeting with Lord Chiddester, and I didn't want to be late."

"You really think Henry is going to believe that?"

"No, but he doesn't need to believe it. He needs to prove it's a lie, and he can't. And he won't want to."

She sighed.

I said, "You said you could forgive anything except infidelity and cutting you out. Can you forgive this?"

She sagged back in her chair and put something that was related to a smile on her face. She gestured at me with both hands. "What? What am I supposed to do? Or say? You know as well as I do that if I had found Mick Harragan alive, back when we first met, I would have blown his brains out without a second thought." She stared at her cup. "And I could never have brought

Maria in. It's like you say, Stone. Sometimes the law doesn't cover the details."[1]

I gave a small laugh and stuffed half a croissant in my mouth. "The crazy thing is, I don't believe in that. It shouldn't be that way."

"I know. But it is. Sometimes you have to believe something, even when you don't believe *in* it. Because . . ." She wagged her finger at me across the table. "Morality, Stone, is a human construct. Let's go."

I drained my coffee, stood, and we headed for the lobby.

Outside, it was already getting warm. The U.K. was caught in a heat wave that the oil industry had given up pretending had nothing to do with climate change. If the planet wasn't getting hotter, England sure was.

We made it to New Scotland Yard through heavy, grinding traffic and got there by nine thirty. Henry was waiting for us on the sidewalk. He didn't look happy. I pulled up beside him and lowered the window. He didn't smile.

"Get out. I'll drive. Carmen, you get in the back. I need to talk to this character."

We played musical chairs for a bit. Dehan climbed in the back and I got in the passenger seat. He got behind the wheel and we took off slow down the Victoria Embankment, following the same route we had followed the day before.

"I am not going to mince words with you, John. And believe me, if it weren't for the years of friendship we have, and because of what happened to Hattie, you would be on the next flight out of here back to New York. But you are going to hear what I bloody well have to say to you, and you are going to take it, or you can fuck off back home."

He turned to look at me. I gave him the dead eye and he carried on.

"We do *not* have gun law in this country. We do *not* allow

---

1. See *An Ace and a Pair*.

coppers to go around beating up civilians. We like it that way, and if we catch a copper trying to take the law into his own hands we come down on him, or her, like a ton of fucking bricks! Whether he is a friend or not. In this country the law is the law, for Brad Johnson, Hattie Stone, you, me, and Lord Chiddester. No exceptions! Step over the line once more, John, and I will have you! Is that understood?"

I nodded. "Perfectly, Henry, and I appreciate that you had to lay it on the line like that. And, believe it or not, in ninety percent of the U.S.A., it's the same." I spread my hands. "However, I want you to be able to look your bosses in the eye and tell them, with a clear conscience, that it went down the way I said. I had questions for him about his alibi. I felt if we spoke in his apartment rather than in the middle of an exhibition hall, he might be more willing to speak. The door was open, and he was lying on the floor, semiconscious. I called you, cleaned him up a bit, and left when I heard the sirens because I was aware my presence could be an embarrassment to your department."

He scowled at me a moment, then sighed. "Fair enough. Sorry about chewing you out. But it can't happen, you know?"

"Hey, I would have done the same if you'd come over to the Bronx and started beating up some of my hard cases." I reached in my pocket and pulled out the freezer bag with the cotton wool in it. I showed it to him and, without cracking a smile, I said, "I asked him if he would mind providing a sample and he said that was fine. I am willing to testify to that, if necessary."

He shook his head. "You son of a bitch," he said, then burst out laughing. "You dirty son of a bitch!"

Dehan spoke up from the back. "I've been checking on Google. You have a private clinic in South London that will do same-day private DNA profiles. Then it's just a matter of comparing the profile that was done fifteen years ago, from the skin under Hattie's fingernails, and the profile we get from this clinic."

He was quiet for a good two or three minutes. Finally, he said, "This is damn close to vigilante behavior. I don't like it. I don't condone it. But I'll have a bike come over and collect the stuff and deliver it to the clinic. And you promise me, you give me your word, that this is the end of it."

I nodded. "You have my word, Henry, but you need to know something. Johnson is not your man for Katie Ellison's killing. You know that as well as I do. And he isn't your man for the other four either."

"What's your point?"

He pulled into Little College Street and parked opposite a tall, elegant Georgian house. He killed the engine and turned to face me.

"I have asked my inspector to pull strings back home and have Johnson extradited. I want him tried in Arizona. U.S. law says it has jurisdiction over any U.S. citizen who commits a crime, anywhere in the world."

He was frowning and looked mad. "This isn't some Third-World banana republic, you know. Our legal system is second to none..."

I sighed. "Come on, Henry! You know that's not the reason. In fact, it's almost the opposite of the reason..."

"What's that supposed to mean?"

Dehan spoke up again. "He means your courts are too lenient. If he is tried in his home state of Arizona, the death penalty will be available. It has been applied thirty-seven times in the last sixty years. And even if he doesn't get the injection, life, for a murder involving rape and torture, will mean life."

He looked embarrassed.

I shrugged. "You know as well as I do, Henry, here he could be out in seven years. You were there. You know what he did to her. You saw the ME's report. He has to pay for that. Then I... *we*... me and Dehan, can put this behind us and get on with our lives."

He was quiet for a while, then finally said, "I can understand that. It's not up to me. It's up to the Home Office and the courts. I just hope you're right, and this does give you closure." He managed half a smile. "Come on, let's go and talk to this knob."

SEVEN

We were shown into Lord Chiddester's office by his secretary. The room was more like a Georgian drawing room than an office. There was a lot of oak, none of it less than three hundred years old, and a lot of well-preserved stucco of about the same age. It was wall-to-wall carpeted, which most British aristocrats frown upon, but it was Wilton and very dark blue with a touch of gold, so I guess that was okay. One wall was taken up by an imposing bookcase with leaded glass panes, and the other walls had prints of horses.

For a moment, as we stepped into the room, I had the surreal sensation that Lord Chiddester was part of the furniture. He was seated behind a magnificent, dark oak desk in a magnificent, dark burgundy leather chair, staring at us, immobile from under his brows. He didn't say anything, he just watched us approach his desk and scowled.

Henry cleared his throat. "My Lord, thank you for agreeing to see us. I wonder if you would be prepared to answer a few questions..."

"Well, I didn't invite you here to discuss the weather, Inspector. What do you want to know?"

Henry loosened his collar. "I understand, sir, that your daughter was writing an article..."

"Probably. What of it?"

"I understand it may have been quite a controversial article and that she may have approached you for some, er..."

"Some what, Inspector? Good lord, man! Spit it out! Is this the best Scotland Yard can come up with? No wonder the bloody country is overrun with damned Islamic terrorists!"

I saw Henry flush and start speaking again. "I understand she may have approached you for some guidance and information, sir?"

Chiddester frowned at him. "Where'd you get that idea? Who told you that?"

"Um, Miss Ellison's housemate, sir, Sarah."

"What else did she tell you?"

Dehan turned and looked at me. She had that expression on her face where she narrowed her eyes, and you knew she was getting mad and wouldn't be able to keep her mouth shut. She spoke in a loud voice as she tied her hair in a knot at the base of her neck.

"You know what, Stone? My dad always brought me up to believe there was nothing so fine and elegant as an English gentleman. 'They are never,' he used to say to me, 'boorish, ill-mannered, or crude. Especially the aristocracy.' That's what he used to say to me. 'They would never, for example, stay sitting down while there was a woman standing.' What do you think of that, Stone?"

I pulled a face and shook my head. "I think he was living in the past, Dehan. Those were the good old days, when England was England, before the European Union, and all the Muslim immigrants. What do you say, Lord Chiddester? Is the English gentleman a dying breed?"

He ignored me and kept his eyes on Dehan. Henry had closed his. Chiddester stood. "Madam, forgive me. That was unforgivable. Will you please sit?" He turned a baleful glare on Green and on me and gestured to two more chairs. Dehan sat and we followed suit. Chiddester scowled at Henry. "Are you going to introduce these people, Inspector?"

"Detectives John Stone and . . ."

Dehan cut in, "Detective Carmen Dehan, we are from the NYPD consulting on your daughter's case."

He sat back. "Dehan?"

"Yes, sir."

"You are of Jewish ancestry?"

"Is that a problem?"

He gave a small laugh. "You are obviously not familiar with U.K. politics at present, Detective Dehan. You will find plenty of anti-Semitism among the Marxists in the Labour Party, but none in my office. I sometimes wonder if those cretins realize that Marx was Jewish." He turned back to Henry, who was looking very confused. "Why is the NYPD being consulted on my daughter's murder, Inspector?"

I sighed noisily while Henry hesitated. Then I got bored and spoke. "Katie's murder, sir, fit the MO of four murders that were committed in Whitechapel fifteen years ago. I was involved in that investigation because I was on an exchange program between the NYPD and Scotland Yard. I think it's fair to say, Lord Chiddester, that nobody knows more about those murders than I do."

"I see."

"And I can tell you that your daughter was not murdered by the same man who killed those four girls."

"You know this how?"

"The man who killed those girls all those years ago was probably an American, and he was most certainly obsessed with Don McLean, a singer from the seventies."

"I know who Don McLean is, Detective."

"The man who killed your daughter was English, and not familiar with Don McLean. It seems like a trivial detail, but put in context, it is irrefutable."

He stared at me for a long moment. Then Dehan spoke up

again. "Sir, with the greatest respect in the world, we are not going to solve your daughter's murder by answering your questions. We already know the answers to the questions you're asking us. We are going to solve this murder by asking *you* questions, and by you getting on board and answering them."

I smiled and watched Henry turn white. Chiddester turned to face her and raised an eyebrow. "Quite so," he said.

"So, did Katie ask you for help relating to an article she was writing?"

He sucked his teeth and drummed his fingers on the arm of his chair. "She called me about three weeks ago. I don't remember exactly. She was very enthusiastic about a project she had. She was mad about the idea of becoming a journalist. She was staunchly right wing, and keen to do something about the sad state of affairs in this country. We talked, I can't remember exactly what about, this and that, the Brexit fiasco, the problem of Islam . . . the usual stuff."

"Did she ask you, can you remember, did she ask you for help or advice?"

He kept his eyes on the desk. "Not that I can recall, no."

I said, "She had been dating a young man called Mark . . ."

He sighed. "On and off, yes. Bit of a drip, long hair, always apologizing. Good family, but no guts. You know the sort."

I nodded like I knew the sort. "But recently she had stopped seeing him. Were you aware of any other romantic involvement in her life?"

His cheeks colored and there was no mistaking the building rage in his eyes. "Yes!" he said. "And I suppose there is no way around this. She had got herself a Muslim boyfriend. I told her she was insane, for any number of reasons, but she told me she was certain he had ties to God knows what, and she was going to use him to get information for her *project*, as she called it. I told her again and again that she was playing with fire. And here we are." He glanced at me. I realized I was making a face of skepticism. He said, "You disagree?"

"I don't know. It just seems odd that a jihadist would go to the trouble of disguising the murder of a British Lord's daughter to make it look like a fifteen-year-old serial killing. It's not only unlikely that he would know the details of those killings, but you'd think the propaganda value would have him and his associates falling over themselves to claim responsibility." I gestured at him. "Especially as you are known in this country for your anti-Islamic stance."

He thought for a moment. "I take your point. It is a good point."

"What's this guy's name?"

"Sadiq Hassan." He flipped open a diary on his desk, scrawled something on a piece of paper, and slid it across to me. It was an address. I handed it to Henry, who took it without speaking.

Chiddester went on. "She assured me she wasn't sleeping with the grubby little fellow, but just wanted to get information out of him. She had the idea he was some kind of terrorist. A refugee, not born here. She wanted me to have MI5 look into him. Perhaps I should have. She was still a child at heart. Poor Katie . . ."

There was a spasm of pain across his face, but it vanished as soon as it appeared. Then he frowned at Dehan. "You married?"

She pointed at me. "To that man over there."

I smiled blandly. "This is our honeymoon."

He grunted. "Pity," he said ambiguously. "Where are you staying?"

"The Ritz."

His eyes went wide. "The Yard is putting you up at the Ritz?" He turned to stare at Henry. "No wonder the country is going to the dogs!" He turned back to me. "But if I need to contact you, I can find you at the Ritz, can I?"

I muttered something about it being a long story and handed him my card. "You have my cell phone there, and my email."

"If I think of anything, I'll let you know. Meantime, you should talk to that Hassan chap. He's your man."

We were being invited to leave. We stood and he stood with us. "My secretary will see you out."

We didn't speak on the way out, but Henry pulled his cell from his pocket and made a call. As we stepped into the humid heat of the gray midmorning, he started to talk.

"Yeah, DI Henry Green here. I need a dispatch rider, Little College Street. Going to Union Road, SW8. Very urgent."

Dehan sat on the hood of his car, looking at him. A brief gust of cool wind came in off the river, and far off a barge moaned. He gave us a humorless smile and said, "Well, that went well, didn't it?"

Dehan shrugged. "I'm sorry, Henry. I knew he was sympathetic to the Israelis. He was being a pain in the ass and we were getting nowhere. I thought it was worth a shot. Guys like that, sometimes you have to bust their balls a bit."

"No, you're quite right. I let him walk all over me. I invited you to consult on this case because you're good. I can't really complain when you, um . . . do your thing, can I?"

I looked up at the seagulls wheeling overhead under the gray sky and asked, "What do you want to do next? You want to see this Sadiq guy alone?"

He gave a small sigh. "No, I think I'd rather like to let Carmen loose on him."

We all managed a smile, and a short while later, the police dispatch rider pulled into the street. Henry went to talk to him and give him the bag of cotton wool buds, and I gave Dehan a smile that was rueful.

She said, "I'm sorry, Stone. He's your friend."

"After today, I'm not so sure. I think I have strained that friendship pretty much to breaking point. I think we may soon get thanked politely and invited to return to New York."

She grimaced. "Is that my fault?"

I shook my head. "No, what I did this morning was beyond the pale. I knew it would be, but I had to do it. This was just the cherry on the cake. I was surprised. Fifteen years ago, he would have taken Chiddester apart."

She squinted at him down the road, where he was talking to the dispatch rider. The breeze caught her hair, and for a moment I thought how lucky I was to have this second chance. "I guess it's easy to be brave when you're young, and you haven't much to lose. Maybe he's married." She looked up at me. "Maybe he has kids, school fees, a mortgage, all those things that sap your heroism and make your boss so powerful."

I nodded. Maybe she was right. I had no idea.

He turned and started walking back toward us. I didn't know if he had married, if he had kids or a mortgage, and it struck me as ironic that I knew so much about the man whom I hated, who had killed my wife and almost destroyed me, and yet I knew so little about the man I had once considered my closest friend.

"Right, chaps," he said. "That's on its way. We'll have the results this evening. They'll email me. Good enough?"

"Superb."

"Shall we go an' see this 'grubby little fellow' then?"

We climbed in the car and slammed the doors. He fired up the engine, and as he pulled away, I said, "We've been here over two weeks, and the only times we've seen you have been when somebody got murdered. We should get together before we leave and have a meal."

He nodded and smiled. He knew what I was doing, and it was okay. "That'd be nice."

"You married? We lost touch. I don't know what you've been doing these past years."

He was silent for a moment, then burst out laughing. He pointed a finger at me. "You are forbidden from speaking for the rest of the day. Do *not* open your mouth again! Every time you open your mouth, you put your sodding foot in it!"

"What did I do?"

He shook his head. "She's talking about divorce. I'm telling her not to. The kids are at a critical age, twelve and thirteen. We married just after you left. It's a time when a lot of couples go through a difficult patch. I want us to see it through. We still like each other, you know. We have a lot to fight for . . ." He paused. We pulled out onto Millbank and headed west. "But she complains about the job, the hours, she has no support . . . She's right. She has a point. But what can I do? I can't be in two places at the same time, and I can't just magically go into another job that pays double and is half as demanding, can I?"

He looked at me as though he thought I might have an answer. Dehan's voice came from the back. "Boy, you are on fire today, Stone."

I made a face. "That's why I married a cop."

He didn't answer. I knew what he was thinking: *Not the first time, you didn't.* And I wondered, what would have happened to my ideal love affair, to my perfect marriage, if she had lived? If she hadn't been murdered? Would we have made it? Or would the stresses and tensions of time and work have started to show, and tell? Would children and long hours have come between us? Would that romantic passion of being in love have faded over time and become mere love, and then friendship, and then not even that, but simply the bonds of familiarity—even contempt? Would she have met someone else? Would I have met Dehan? And if I had . . .

I blinked. None of that happened, because she was killed. And then I met Dehan—and her attitude. I said, "If you feel it's worth fighting for, Henry, fight for it. Woo her, romance her, rekindle the fire, sacrifice the job if you have to, get transferred to a nine till five desk. Nothing is more important than your family."

I saw him glance in the mirror at Dehan. I heard her say, "He's right, Henry. Family is where it's at."

And we moved on along the river, toward Whitechapel, and Sadiq Hassan.

EIGHT

WE ARRIVED SHORTLY BEFORE LUNCHTIME. HE HAD A small, two-story house on the corner of Duckett Street and Bale Road, opposite a large building site that sported a billboard written entirely in Arabic. In the window, there was a large red poster showing a fist clenching a sickle. In black letters it said *Whitechapel Marxist Party*. Henry rang the bell and I saw a figure peer through the window. A moment later, the door opened halfway and a young man in his midtwenties peered out. He looked Mediterranean, with thick black hair, dark eyes, and olive skin. He was unshaven and barefoot, in black jeans and a black T-shirt with the same logo as his poster, only in white.

Henry said, "Sadiq Hassan?"

"Who are you?"

He had an accent, but it wasn't strong. Henry showed him his badge. "Detective Inspector Henry Green, these are Detectives Stone and Dehan, who are accompanying me. Are you Sadiq Hassan?"

"What if I am?"

"If you are, then we'd like to ask you some questions, sir."

"What about?"

"Well, sir, if you're not Sadiq Hassan, that's none of your business, is it? So once again, *are* you Sadiq Hassan?"

Five seconds of silence in a conversation is a long time. He took at least that long to stare at each one of us. He took a couple of seconds longer with Dehan before he answered, and echoed Chiddester's question, but with a different tone to his voice.

"Dehan?"

She raised an eyebrow at him. "Yeah, it's Irish."

He opened the door the full way and leaned on the jamb. "I am Sadiq Hassan. So what?" His eyes strayed to Dehan again and he gave her the once-over.

Henry ignored his manner and asked him, "Do you know a young lady, name of Katie Ellison?"

He didn't answer. He looked at Henry's shoes, then his pants. His face said they were the most disgusting shoes and pants he'd ever seen. Then he looked at his shirt in the same way, and finally at his face.

"Why you askin' me about this fuckin' bitch?" I felt Dehan stiffen and put my hand on her arm. "You come to my house, askin' about this whore? Why you come to my house askin' about this whoring bitch?"

"Why don't we do something, Mr. Hassan? Why don't I ask the questions, and you provide the answers? Now, once again. Do you know Katie Ellison?"

He curled his lip and nodded. "Yeah, I know Katie Ellison. She is a fuckin' whoring bitch. What else you want to know?"

Henry pulled out a notebook and a pencil. "When was the last time you saw her?"

"Week ago."

"Where did you see her?"

"At a meeting of the WMP. The lying bitch said she wanted to be a member and get involved. She was fuckin' lying, innit?"

I scratched my chin. "How do you know she was lying?"

"I looked in her bag. She had a digital recorder, with interviews on it. She'd been recording our fuckin' meetin's. She was writin' some kind of fuckin' article, innit? Some kind of fuckin' exposé." He turned his head and looked Dehan in the face. "Plus she was fuckin' some Jew. Dirty bitch. How any woman can fuck a Jew, she must be a filthy whore, I tell you."

I kept my voice real quiet. "You better keep a civil tongue in your head, Sadiq."

He smiled. "Oh yeah? The big American, coming here threatening the Arabs again. What you gonna do? Bomb my house? Fuck you!"

Henry spoke loudly. "Where was this meeting, Mr. Hassan?"

"In my house."

"Was there an altercation?"

Sadiq was quiet and still for a long moment.

"Do you understand the question, Mr. Hassan? Did you have a..."

"Yeah! I understand the fuckin' question! I told her to get out! I tried to take her recorder, because I reckon the stuff on it was mine and belonged to me, innit? But she fought me, and Bernard, some English piece of shit secretary of the party, held me back and she left. That was the last time I seen her. You should go and get the fuckin' recorder from her, if you was proper police!"

"Have you got an address for her?"

"Yeah, Halcrow Street."

Henry nodded. "That's just up the road, right?"

"Yeah."

"Did you go and visit her afterwards, to try again to get the recordings back?"

Sadiq frowned. "No. Why?"

"We are almost done, Mr. Hassan. Just one more question. Are you familiar with the Butcher of Whitechapel?"

Sadiq's eyes narrowed. He spoke cautiously. "Somethin', why?"

Henry put the notebook and the pencil back in his pocket. "Why?" he said. "Why? Because Katie Ellison was found raped and murdered yesterday, Mr. Hassan, in her flat on Halcrow

Street. And I'm wondering if you would be willing to give us samples of your DNA and fingerprints, so we can compare them with samples found at the scene. What do you say, Mr. Hassan?"

His face had turned a pasty gray. He was shaking his head. "No, no . . . No way. This is harassment because I'm a Muslim . . ."

Henry sighed. "We will be back with a warrant, Mr. Hassan. If we are going to find your DNA and prints at the scene, you're better off telling us now and explaining why. Lies won't help you."

His eyes were swiveling from me to Dehan and back to Henry again. "Okay, come in, but just the living room. You cannot go anywhere else. That is my family in there. You stay away from them."

He led us into a small, dingy living room with a TV, two cheap sofas, and a shelf with two books: *Islamic Marxism* and the Koran. Sadiq sat on the sofa opposite the TV. Henry and I sat on the other, and Dehan remained standing with her arms crossed.

"We was seein' each other for a couple of weeks, right? So I went to her place a couple of times and we had sex. So you're going to find my prints and my DNA there, most likely. But I didn't kill her." His face kind of twisted and he said, "It would be no crime if I had, in Sharia. And you will incorporate Sharia into British law, you'll see. She *said* she converted, but it was a lie, and she was havin' sex with a Jew while she was saying she was my woman. She deserved to die for that, in the eyes of Allah! But I didn't kill her."

I saw Henry's face flush. "Unfortunately for you, Mr. Hassan, this country doesn't operate under Sharia law. And under the laws of the United Kingdom, you can convert as often as you like to whatever religion you like, and you can have sex with whomever you please. We'll leave it to the jury to decide whether you killed Miss Ellison or not." He stood and I stood with him. "I'll be back with a warrant for your DNA."

He stared at us with wide eyes as we moved toward the door.

As we were stepping out, Dehan looked at him like he was crazy. "Do you know *anything* about Karl Marx?" He just stared. He didn't answer. "You know he was a Jew, right? You know he created Marxism in the first place to protect Jews against German and Austrian anti-Semitism, right?" She shook her head and stepped out the door, muttering, "Dumb asshole."

As we reached the car and climbed in, he shouted from the door, pointing at Dehan. "You're a racist! You called me an asshole because I am a Muslim!"

She paused, halfway in the car. "No, I called you an asshole because you're an asshole, asshole."

We climbed in and closed the doors. Henry was on the radio. "I need a twenty-four-hour watch on Sadiq Hassan as of now. I want to know where he goes, who he sees, who he talks to, what he eats, drinks, where he *shits*! Everything!"

The radio crackled and a girl's voice said, "Literally, boss?"

"No, not literally, Karen..."

"Didn't think so, sir. Everything apart from where he shits, then?"

"Yes, Karen, everything apart from that."

"Right you are, boss."

I said, "He didn't do it."

"I know. I wish he had, though, nasty piece of work. But he reacted all wrong to my question about the Butcher..."

Dehan spoke up from the back. "And if he had killed her, he would have made sure the whole world knew why. The Butcher of Whitechapel has no meaning for him."

I sucked my teeth and asked nobody in particular, "So who's this Jewish guy she was seeing?"

A dark blue Ford Mondeo rolled past and Henry suddenly fired up the engine and pulled away. "They're here," he said. "I need to talk to CID. This whole thing is getting way out of hand. One thing is clear..."

I glanced at him. "What?"

"You were right from the start. This has nothing to do with the Butcher of Whitechapel."

I made a face and a long "Hmmm..." noise.

He looked at me sharply. "Don't tell me you now think it *has*!"

I could hear Dehan sniggering in the back. "You are such a pain in the ass, Stone..."

"The killing was not committed by the same guy. But that is not the same as saying they are not connected. There is a connection."

Henry was shaking his head. "No. This is political." We drove in silence for a while. He chewed his lip, leaning forward slightly over the steering wheel. "That was a purely psychosexual motivation: some dark, Freudian need to punish his mother or something equally unedifying. This is political. The motivation is totally different. I'll drop you back at the hotel."

We didn't talk again until we had arrived at Piccadilly and he'd pulled up outside the hotel. As we were about to climb out, he said, "I'll be in touch after I've spoken to the chaps at CID. Enjoy London for the afternoon. Let's have dinner soon."

We thanked him and he drove away.

Dehan said, "He's giving us the shove."

I watched his car disappear into the traffic. "Yup."

"Do you care?"

I looked at her and nodded. "Yup."

"Why?"

"Because he's got it wrong."

She shrugged and sighed. "Well, it's not our case, Stone. So what do you want to do this afternoon?"

I smiled at her. "In this order, have a prelunch martini in the bar, a light lunch in the dining room, and then we'll go and see Lord Chiddester, probably at his country house in West Sussex."

She thumped me on the chest. "Come on, Stone! Give it up!" We started toward the door and the doorman opened it for us.

"The first two sound great. The third is dumb. You've been told to leave it alone. They've got this."

We stepped into the cool, elegant lobby and moved toward the cocktail bar. "I am not going to do anything, Dehan, except accept His Lordship's invitation."

"Really?"

"You shall regret your sarcastic tone. You see if you don't."

We had negotiated to potted palms and were now in the dark cool of the cocktail bar. I signaled the waiter. "Two martinis, very dry . . ." I smiled. "Shaken, not stirred."

Dehan turned her back on the bar and leaned her elbow on it. "Okay, Stone, John Stone, what makes you so sure Lord Chiddester is going to invite us to West Sussex?"

"Because he asked how he could contact us, and he is on his way to Chiddester even as we speak, to be with his wife. He's a hard man who doesn't show his feelings, but he is also a passionate man of strict morals who wants his daughter's killer caught. He believes Muslims are involved, he doesn't trust Henry to do the job, but he is impressed by you, and *our attitude* to the case. He also reasons that we are not bound by the police code of conduct. He will have his secretary contact us in the next hour, and probably send a car. Perhaps a Rolls or a Bentley."

"In your dreams, pal. Even if you were right, how can you know that he'll do that in the next hour? You're showing off."

I shook my head. The barman poured the two martinis and I handed one to Dehan and sipped the other. "He's no fool. He's a smart man. He saw how we, and in particular you, made Henry look bad. He knows that before long, Henry is going to thank us politely and send us on our merry ways, so he will be keen to talk to us and see if we can help him before that happens."

She made a face and nodded once. "Huh." Then she shrugged. "We'll see. You think Henry is right and this is politically motivated?"

I spent a while bobbing the olive up and down in my glass. Eventually, I said, "The killing is political, but probably with a small *p*. I mean that she was not killed because she was right wing, but because she was becoming a threat to somebody's position. But the killing is also connected to the original murders somehow. I figure our original, genuine serial killer is either dead or in prison somewhere. I am pretty sure of that. But there is a missing link that somehow connects him to Katie Ellison. That link, between the original killer and Katie, will show us who her real killer is, and why he chose to emulate the Butcher."

"What kind of link?"

I shook my head. "That is where I keep drawing a blank. It's something obvious, simple . . ."

"Hidden in plain sight."

"Hidden in plain sight. Exactly."

She sipped her martini, then smacked her lips. "Sadiq had plenty of motive. All that hatred and vitriol. It wouldn't be hard to whip him up into a homicidal rage."

I held the thought in my mind for a moment. "His motive was there, but he wasn't. Given time, he might have done it, but he didn't."

"I bet he can't spell whiskey."

I smiled. My phone rang. I winked at Dehan and she rolled her eyes.

"Yeah, Stone."

"Stone, it's Lord Chiddester here. Look, sorry I wasn't more forthcoming this morning. That man Green is a hopeless incompetent. No spine, no guts, and no balls . . ."

"That's a lot of anatomy he's missing, Lord Chiddester." I smiled at Dehan.

"Quite so. Now, I'd like to talk to you and your partner, Dehan, privately. I am fully prepared to remunerate you adequately. I am sending a car for you at the Ritz. I thought we could have drinks and a chat, with my wife, and then you could dine here with us and I'll have my driver take you back to London in the morning. Would that be acceptable?"

I raised an eyebrow and held Dehan's eye. "That would be fine. What time will your driver be here, sir?"

"Well, I thought after luncheon, in about an hour and a half?"

"After lunch would be perfect. I look forward to it, sir."

"Splendid, I'll see you later then."

"Yup. See you later."

I hung up. "Do I look smug?"

She nodded. "Uh-huh."

"That's because I feel smug." I turned to the barman and made the victory sign at him. "Let's have another before lunch."

NINE

We were picked up after lunch by a chauffeur in a uniform, driving a classic, dark blue Bentley S3, from 1965, when Bentleys and Rolls-Royces really looked like Bentleys and Rolls-Royces. We didn't so much climb in the back as walk in and take our seats in a small drawing room. As we cruised over the river, Dehan looked around at the walnut panels and the leather upholstery and asked, "Is this what life is going to be like with you, Stone?"

There was a hint of irony in her smile. I didn't answer, vaguely aware that it was mainly because of her that we were in that car, going where we were going.

The drive took about an hour and a half, through green fields, woodlands, and hedgerows that would have been nauseating on a chocolate box, but in the real world elevated prettiness to something beyond words. We drove past Arundel Castle, silhouetted against the afternoon sky on the South Downs, skirted by the River Arun and flanked by dense woodlands.

Finally, as we began to glimpse the misty haze of the English Channel in the south, we turned in through a set of large, crested iron gates and wound through lush parkland down a gravel drive that seemed to be in no particular hurry to reach the magnificent

Tudor manor house at the end. It was large, half-timbered in parts and redbrick in others, with tall chimney pots and cantilevered windows with small, diamond-shaped leaded panes. It was the kind of place, I told myself, I'd go to after I died, if I had been very, very good. I glanced at Dehan.

She had her narrow eyes on. "I thought this was just in the movies," she said. "I didn't think anybody lived like this anymore."

The great beast eased to a stop outside a door that was older than my country, and a butler of about the same age stepped out to receive us. He gave a small bow and said, "My Lord Chiddester is in his study, if you would care to follow me . . ."

He led us across heavy oak floors through an oak-paneled drawing room with a fireplace as big as my house, and tapped on another ancient oak door. A muted voice called, "Come!" and he stepped in.

"Detectives Stone and Dehan, M'Lord."

Chiddester's disembodied voice said, "Good. Show them in, Trout!"

Trout stepped aside and held the door for us. I followed Dehan in. The study wasn't huge. It was no more than twenty feet square, with a leaded window at either end and a large fireplace in the middle, to the right of his desk. The window frames were heavy, solid beams of wood. The floors were bare boards, darkened and smoothed by the passage of centuries, and the ceiling was supported by massive wooden rafters. A low dresser held the obligatory decanters, and two bookcases held the necessary books. The room smelled of pipe tobacco, and the chairs he indicated as we came in were ancient, cracked, extremely comfortable Chesterfields. His face was drawn and colorless, but he attempted to smile.

"Dehan, Stone, please come in and sit. Can I offer you a drink? Perhaps a whiskey . . . ?"

We told him that would do fine. He splashed a couple of

inches into a couple of cut crystal tumblers that weighed about half a pound each and returned to his chair, behind the desk.

I began to speak, "Lord Chiddester..."

"Just Chiddester, please, I think we can dispense with the formalities."

I nodded and smiled, and tried to get my mouth around it like it was a name. "Chiddester, I think we are going to be given our marching orders by DI Green before very long. I am not sure how helpful we can be to you."

He waved my comment aside. "You don't need his permission to stay in the country. And if you're acting for me, you can stay as long as you like."

"I appreciate the offer. But we do need to get back to work. Unfortunately, we answer to our chief..."

He smiled, and there was a wicked edge to it that said he was used to getting what he wanted, and he liked it that way.

"Inspector John Newman, of the Forty-Third Precinct, isn't it?" He laughed at my expression. "Don't worry, Stone, all I ask is that you hear me out, and Fi, my wife." The laughter drained from his face. "I'm very much afraid Green is galloping off on the wrong track on this thing." He turned his eyes on Dehan and I noticed for the first time how blue they were, and how intense his stare was. "I want my daughter avenged, Dehan. You understand that, don't you? She was everything to us. We're a close family. Not given to public exhibitions, wailing and thrashing. But we were close. Are close. And this killer, whoever he is, has taken my daughter from me. I want him caught. And I don't trust Green to do the job."

"Okay." I sighed. "So what didn't you tell us at your office this morning?"

He turned his eyes on me and for a moment, his face reminded me of a hawk, or an eagle. "I am conservative, right wing. I don't give a damn what your politics are. That's your business. But I am right wing. I believe, passionately, in democracy, small government, and our ancient liberties. They are the same as your ancient liberties. You inherited them from us." He paused, staring into his glass. "I despise Fascism, Socialism, Communism, and Islam: any doctrine that robs an individual of his freedom. I may seem to be going 'round the houses." He raised his eyes to look at me under his brows. "But these are facts you need to know and understand."

He sipped his whiskey and seemed to organize his next thoughts while he savored it.

"I don't hate these ideologies in an arbitrary fashion. I hate them because I have studied them in depth and I believe them to be evil and inhuman. I am nominally an Anglican, a Protestant, but I am probably an atheist and don't actually give a damn about religion. I am not pro-Jewish." He turned to gaze at Dehan. "I am pro-Israel, because I believe that in a world that is going steadily insane, Israel is a small bastion of sanity and civilization. I am not a racist. I despise German Nazism as much as I despise Arab Islam. There's bugger all to tell between them, frankly. Is all that clear?"

"Abundantly."

He looked at Dehan. She had her eyebrows raised, but she nodded.

He asked, "Can you live with it?"

She said, "It depends what you mean by 'live.' What do you want us to do with it, besides understand it?"

"Nothing. Just understand it. Understand that and you start to understand Katie. Katie was the same. She and I had very much the same views. She was sound, immensely patriotic, not nationalistic in the European sense. Damned Europeans never could get anything right. It has nothing to do with being racially superior or any of that bloody nonsense. She just believed in England, and loved it.

"Like me, she deplored what the Communists and the Socialists have done to it, she deplored what the European Union has done to it, and she deplored the way one damned government after another has sold our country to Islam in exchange for oil.

She was very outspoken, courageous, and I was very proud of her for that."

I was listening hard, trying to sift through his barely controlled passions to find what he was actually driving at. I said, "Are you saying that you think she was killed because of her views?"

He shook his head. "Not directly."

"You'll have to explain that."

He stood and walked to the ancient, leaded window and stood looking out at the lawns and rosebushes outside. "There are people, on both sides of the House, Socialists *and* conservatives, who will go to any lengths to bow to pressure from Islamic countries, who accommodate any number of immigrants and refugees, build any number of mosques, and justify any number of atrocities, simply because they control most of the world's oil reserves." He paused and sipped his drink. "You've had scandals in your own country, as we have here, where political figures have been caught making arms deals in which British or American weapons have ended up in the hands of ISIS or the Taliban or Al-Qaeda."

He turned to face us. "But what Katie was worried about went a lot further. What had Katie terrified was that there are Al-Qaeda cells in this country with close ties to Communist and Marxist parties that have, in turn, ties to the Labour Party, to the very establishment itself. Her project, as she called it, was to expose those ties, through a series of articles in a major, national paper, and wake the country up to what was happening in Parliament, in the Commons and the Lords."

He paused, staring down at his feet. "Her theory was more radical than that. She claimed this sickness had spread all across Europe and the U.S.A. She may well be right, but her focus was England. And so is mine."

Dehan winced. "That sounds pretty paranoid."

He smiled at her without much humor. "If it were paranoia, Dehan, she would have committed suicide. But she didn't. She was murdered."

She stared at him, taking in what he'd said, then asked, "This was what she phoned you about the other night?"

"Yes. I didn't want to discuss this in front of Green. He'd've thought I'd taken leave of my senses. I have no love of Islam, as you know, but at first, even I thought Katie was indulging in conspiracy theory nonsense. However, when she started showing me the evidence . . ."

I frowned. "What evidence?"

He paced over to the fireplace and stood with one hand resting on the massive beam that constituted the mantelpiece, the other holding his glass. He gazed down into the cold soot and said, "You've probably never heard of Justin Caulfield. He's a shadow cabinet minister, dyed-in-the-wool communist, all for disarmament, giving up our nuclear weapons, getting out of NATO, give the Falklands to the ruddy Argies. Unspeakable man. Managed to get into the shadow cabinet and could conceivably become prime minister.

"Well, Katie gathered evidence . . ." He turned his head to look at me. "And I mean photographs, films, recordings, emails . . . the works, showing that Caulfield has close ties not just with the International Communist Party, but with local Marxist parties in the U.K. and with active commanders in Al-Qaeda, *and* with an organization known as the ICP . . ."

Dehan said, "The Islamic Communist Party."

He nodded at her. "Exactly. Was there ever a more absurd or dangerous notion?"

I grunted. "I'm a little confused. We spoke to Sadiq Hassan today, just before coming here. He said your daughter was having an affair with someone he simply referred to as 'a Jew.'" I shrugged. "But according to Sarah, Katie wasn't seeing anybody, she was too involved with her work. On the other hand, according to you, she was seeing Sadiq as part of her investigation." I spread my hands. "Can you clarify that? Have you any idea who Sadiq might be referring to?"

He made a face that suggested he wasn't very interested in the question. Then he returned to his chair.

"You know the tragedy of this whole thing? I have a reputation around this country for being 'pro-Jewish' and 'anti-Arab.' The fact is I have no idea, and even less interest, in what religions, faiths, and ideologies the people I know adhere to. I know my wife is an Anglican because her father insisted we marry in an Anglican church. But ask me about any of my closest friends or family, I don't know and I don't care.

"On the rare occasions my daughter brought a chap home, all I wanted to know was, was he kind to her? Would he make her happy, and could he afford her? In that order." He took a deep breath, held it, and then blew out noisily. "But that hardly answers your question, does it? As far as I was aware, she was not seeing anyone in any serious way. All her focus was on her project, and within that, her target was Justin Caulfield. If I had to hazard a guess, I would have to say she was seeing somebody in Caulfield's employ. But it is very unlikely that anyone in the Labour Party shadow cabinet would employ a Jew. They are deeply and endemically anti-Semitic."

Dehan was chewing her lip. She said unexpectedly, "The Third Reich was about as anti-Semitic as you can get, but Hitler was part Jewish. He just kept it off his résumé."

I smiled. "Fair point."

There was a tap at the door. It opened, and Trout stepped in.

"M'Lord, M'Lady has risen and intends to come down to the drawing room for a cocktail before dinner. She asked me to inform you she will be down in approximately ten minutes."

Chiddester nodded. "Thank you, Trout." Trout withdrew and Chiddester almost managed a smile. "Shall we take our drinks to the drawing room, then? My wife might be able to give you a different perspective from my own. Sometimes she tells me I only knew one side of Katie." He paused, and just for a moment, there was a glimpse of the intolerable pain he was living through. "If that is so," he said, "it is something to be regretted. We should know everything about our children, and we should never outlive them."

He stood abruptly, went and opened the door, and he and I followed Dehan out into the drawing room. The drapes were still open, as were the leaded windows, and a pleasant breeze was coming in, scented with roses and freshly mowed grass. Outside, you could hear the long, complicated song of a blackbird trailing out into the fading evening light.

Chiddester stood in front of the cold fireplace. It was huge, large enough for him to stand inside, and suddenly, despite his strong, vigorous frame, I had the odd feeling that he had somehow aged and shrunk, even since the morning. He gazed down at the large cast-iron grate and said, suddenly, "I should have stopped her. I should have told her it was too dangerous. I should have refused to help."

I didn't know what to say. I knew his feelings only too intimately, but I had nothing to offer him as a remedy. I had never found one. I had never found redemption for Hattie's death. I found instead my attention riveted to the endless song of the blackbird, calling into the encroaching dark.

Dehan watched him a moment, then said, "Could you have stopped her?"

He looked around, sharply, frowning, then seemed to think about what she'd asked him. "Probably not, but I should have tried."

She shrugged. "Speaking as a daughter, who lost her father when I was only small, what kept me going, what still keeps me going, is the knowledge that he and I were on the same page." She hesitated for a fraction of a second. "Maybe I'm impertinent, Chiddester, but we all die. We all have to die sooner or later. But we don't *have* to have somebody who connects with us, who knows who we are in this world, and what we are about, and doesn't try to stop us. You two were lucky. You had that, and she took that with her."

He frowned at her for a long moment. He looked almost

shocked, affronted, but not by Dehan or what she'd said; by life, by a world that could do this to him. He nodded a couple of times, then turned and marched to the door, opened it, and strode out.

Dehan wiped her eye with her fingers. When she spoke, her voice was almost a whisper. "I thought he didn't care. He does, though."

"That was nice, what you said."

She came over and placed her fist gently on my chest. "No one gets out alive, Stone. We know that. So we have to make every moment count. You can't save anybody, not really. But you can help make it worthwhile."

"Are you going philosophical on me, Dehan?"

She didn't smile. "That's not philosophy, Stone. It's just an attitude. It's been a hell of a honeymoon. It makes you think. What is each moment worth? How do you measure its value? Katie, what was she? Twenty-two? Twenty-three? If she had finished her article and published it, and changed the face of British politics, would her life have been more valuable than it is now? Or would it have been more valuable if she had left her research, and lived to a ripe old age and made her parents, her husband, and her children happy? How do you measure the value of a life, Stone?"

Outside, the blackbird went quiet, and inch by inch, the dark closed in. I shook my head. "I don't know," I said. "I don't know."

TEN

THE DOOR OPENED AND A WOMAN STOOD FRAMED IN the ancient Tudor archway. She was in her early fifties, attractive, nicely curvaceous, dressed in a white satin evening gown with a single string of pearls at her throat. Her face was attractive too, but she was drawn and pale, and the makeup around her eyes could not quite conceal the redness or the swelling from where she had been crying. She stood with extraordinary dignity and smiled at us. Her voice, when she spoke, was husky, slightly nasal, as though she had a cold.

"Have you been left alone? That really is too bad of Chiddie. I shall scold him when he gets back."

I stepped forward. "Lady Chiddester. How do you do? I am John Stone. May I present my wife, Carmen?"

She laughed and it was a surprisingly earthy sound, almost like a gurgle of pleasure. "Oh please, we are friends here, and at home. Call me Fiona, or better still, Fi. All that *Downton Abbey* stuff gets so tiresome, don't you agree?" The question was directed at Carmen, who smiled and took her hand but didn't seem to know what to do with it.

So she grinned and said, "Yes, very tiresome." She turned her grin on me. "Isn't that what I'm always telling Mo? 'Enough with the *Downton Abbey* stuff, already!'"

Lady Chiddester, Fi, hooted and smacked Dehan's arm. "I'm going to like you, you're naughty! Now, do you think you can persuade your gorgeous husband to fix me a *very* strong martini, New York style?"

Dehan winked at me. "Make it happen, Stone. Two drinks for the naughty girls."

I found the drinks tray and started mixing a dry martini with what I told myself was a Bronx kicker but was simply an extra dash of vodka. I figured she needed it. Meanwhile, she linked her arm through Dehan's and led her to the sofa.

"I suppose Chiddie has told you everything . . ." They sat, and Fi made a noise that was wistful. "People of our generation don't really show our feelings much, you know. It's not considered the done thing. At least in our circle. God alone knows what everybody else does. I know you Americans positively encourage it. Perhaps you're right to, I don't know, but it does make it awfully hard to cope if you're blubbering all over the place, doesn't it?"

I handed them their drinks and sat in a comfortable old chair opposite.

She smiled her thanks. "Life doesn't get any easier, does it, just because we feel entitled to be upset?"

"I guess it doesn't. Lord Chiddester suggested that you might have a perspective on Katie that he lacked. If you feel up to . . ."

"Oh, goodness, with a couple of your martinis inside me, I'll be up to anything. For heaven's sake, don't be kind." She gazed at the open window for a moment. The last of the light had finally gone beyond the horizon, leaving only an inch of pale glow behind the inky silhouettes of the trees. "Perspective?" she said, vaguely. "I know she would have done anything on Earth to please her father. She adored him." She gave a small, distant smile. "Poor love, she never realized that he felt *exactly* the same way about her." She blinked and seemed to return from a distant place, then turned her watery eyes on me. "No man was ever good enough, naturally, for *either* of them. He is . . ." She sighed. "He is a hard act to follow. There is an awful lot of him, and you tend to get it all at once, without let up. Most men sort of wilt in his presence."

I thought of Henry and couldn't help smiling. "You were aware of her project?"

"Yes." Her face said she had found it distasteful. "She could have done so many things. But they were both obsessed with this national thing, England had to be saved. Not Britain, you understand, Scotland and Wales could sod off. England had to be saved . . . And I suppose they were right, to some extent. But we have paid such a heavy price, and what have we achieved?"

I waited a moment, watching her, then said, "We won't know that until we find who did this. But whatever she did achieve, it will never be enough." She didn't answer, and after a moment, I asked, "You were aware that she had let her relationship with Mark slide . . ."

"Oh!" She waved a hand at me. "That boy! He should have been Italian. The pink lips, permed hair, and those appalling suits. He even wore slip-on shoes without socks! Can you imagine? I don't think there was a drop of testosterone in his body. And men's perfume! I ask you! Surely that is an oxymoron! Men *do not use* perfume! Men smell of *men*!"

Dehan screwed up her face and hugged Fi's arm. I had never seen her do that before. I gave a small laugh and continued with my question. "I'm inclined to agree, Fi, but my question was: she was briefly involved with Sadiq Hassan, but that didn't last, and he claims that she was involved with a Jewish man. Have you any idea who that might have been?"

She rolled her eyes and shook her head. "Honestly, those three religions. You know, Taoists, Buddhists, Shinto . . . unless they are monks and dressed in some peculiar getup, you just don't know when you've met one, do you? But these Judeo-Christians, they are *forever* telling you about their version of God. It's like the whole gay thing. They are forever telling you, and, I mean, I really don't care whom you enjoy sex with or whom you pray to. I have no idea which of my friends are Christian or Jewish, or anything else for that matter. I suspect some of the more interesting ones may be into witchcraft."

I wasn't sure if I was supposed to laugh or not. I drew breath, but Dehan cut me short. "Let me rephrase the question, Fi. Were you aware that Katie was involved with anyone other than Sadiq or Mark?"

She thought about it for a moment, then nodded. "Yes. It's possible. We never pried, you understand. But certain comments she made, I got the impression that she was involved with a man and that she was somewhat ambivalent about him."

"I'm curious," I said, "as to how she indicated she was ambivalent about this man, if she didn't tell you she was involved."

She raised a withering eyebrow at me. "Are you cross-examining me, Mr. Stone?"

I offered her my blandest smile. "Only a little, Fi."

She turned to Dehan. "Isn't he naughty? I see why you like him." She took a sip. "She would speak in generalities and abstractions. 'Do you think it's possible, Mama, to love a man who has no principles?' 'Mama, if you were to fall in love with a man whom you knew to be no good for you, what would *you* do?'"

I nodded. "I get the idea. And are these actual questions she asked you?"

"I'm afraid so."

"How long ago?"

"We last saw her just over two weeks ago."

Dehan sucked her teeth and sat forward, with her elbows on her knees. "Those questions could easily have been about Sadiq."

"Oh, good heavens no! She couldn't *stand* him. Vile little man, that's how she described him. Couldn't bear him!" Dehan and I exchanged a glance and she caught it. "What? Why the secret glance?"

Dehan answered. "He told us they were intimate..."

"He was lying. She was unequivocal about it. She found

everything about him repulsive. She described him as a nasty, revolting bully. He was forever trying to get intimate and she was forever putting him off."

I stared at her. "Forgive me for being blunt, Fi, but this could be very important. Are you absolutely certain you are not . . ." I searched for a polite way of saying it.

She helped me. "Kidding myself? Absolutely not. Katie has been with inappropriate boys a few times in the past and I have just had to live with it. And she has never lied to me. She was adamant about Sadiq. She was stringing him along and, in her words, would not sleep with him if he were the last man on Earth. She actually shuddered when she said it."

I held Dehan's eye.

Fi said, "What are you not telling me?"

The door opened and Chiddester stepped in. "My sincerest apologies. I had some, um, ah, unavoidable business to attend to . . ." He trailed off. His eye flicked from Dehan's face to his wife's and then mine. "I am afraid I have interrupted something."

Fi held out her hand to him. "Not at all, Chiddie, darling. Come and sit down. We were just discussing Katie and that nasty little man Sadiq. I think Stone and Carmen may have something to tell us."

There was something severe in his expression. He raised an eyebrow at me. "Really? Something that didn't come up before?"

He crossed the room and sat, ignoring his wife's hand. I nodded a couple of times.

"When you told us that Katie had not had intimate relations with Sadiq, I'm afraid we both dismissed it as a daughter not sharing intimate details with her parents, and a parent not wanting to see a disagreeable truth. We took this view for a very particular reason."

Dehan took over. "Sadiq was adamant that he and Katie had been intimate. That of itself doesn't mean anything, but when we told him we were testing her sheets, and the whole apartment, for fingerprints and DNA, he became terrified. He told us that we would find his DNA at her apartment, but he swore it was there because they had been intimate. But now, from what you are telling us, that isn't true. So it raises the question, why is his DNA there?"

Her face went like stone and she looked at her husband. "So, Chiddie, it was him, then."

"I hope," I said, looking into my glass, "that you are not intending to do anything rash. Personally, I think your daughter's assessment of Sadiq Hassan was accurate, and I am pretty sure Dehan would agree. But if you make a rash mistake now, you could cause irreparable damage to what your daughter may have achieved."

Chiddester muttered, "What do you mean?"

"First of all, I am pretty certain Sadiq did not kill your daughter. There are unanswered questions about how his DNA got there, but the answer to those questions is *not* that he killed her. So that means, if he didn't, somebody else did. Somebody with a more complex motive, somebody Sadiq Hassan thought was Jewish. Now, if I am right, that could mean that Katie had opened a big can of worms. And if she did, and we handle this investigation right, then her death need not have been in vain. But if you go off half cock and do something rash, you not only end up in jail, you also damage your own cause, and your daughter's sacrifice ends up being for nothing."

He nodded. "You're right. Absolutely right. We'll play it your way for now, but make no mistake, Stone. At some point, somehow, that little shit will pay with his life for what he did to my Katie."

Fi nodded at him. "Hear, hear, spare no expense."

I was spared from having to answer their comments by Trout opening the door behind me and saying, "Dinner is served, M'Lord."

At dinner, they both seemed exhausted, and conversation was stilted and formal in a way that our previous talk had not been. They both made it clear that the discussion about Katie was closed, and the truth was, I didn't think they had anything more to tell us. So we discussed Broadway, a subject about which I know little; the West End, about which I know less; hunting, shooting, and fishing, about which I know absolutely nothing; and the difficulties of being a cold-cases cop in the Bronx, a subject in which they had next to no interest at all, though they both said it was "frightfully interesting."

As soon as we had finished our coffee and cognac, Dehan and I excused ourselves, saying we had to make an early start in the morning, and were shown up to our room by Trout.

It was a sultry night. We had the windows open and all the covers thrown back, save a single sheet. Outside, the moon was brilliant, turning the sky an almost green shade of turquoise. There were birds I could not identify. One may have been a nightingale; the other kept repeating two high-pitched dots, as though sending the message, "I" over and over again in Morse code, echoing into infinity, lost under the moon.

Dehan had her head on my shoulder, with her black hair pressed against my cheek. "This is a very strange place, this archipelago. It has been a very strange honeymoon."

"You want to go home? We don't have to do this."

She shook her head, rubbing her hair into my face. "No, I want to find who killed Katie. I like these people, they're nuttier than squirrel shit, but I like them."

"Nuttier than squirrel shit? Seriously?"

She raised her head to look at me from less than an inch away, so her eyes looked huge. "Yeah, you know, crazier than a soup sandwich."

"Crazy as a cat in a dog factory?"

"Loopy as a cross-eyed cowboy."

"I get it, the wheel's turning but the hamster is dead."

She laid her chin on the backs of her hands on my chest, making her nose and eyes even bigger. I didn't want to tell her, so I stared at the ceiling instead. She said, "Justin Caulfield, an anti-

Semitic Marxist pretending to be a mainstream Socialist. I wonder if we could wangle a visit?"

"We could try. But what would it achieve? This case is beginning to feel very political and very British. I confess the link with the original serial killings is just slipping through my fingers. What are we saying . . . ?"

She sighed. "I know . . ."

"That a man who could be prime minister of Great Britain in a year or two is also a serial killer? And how do we explain the fifteen years of inactivity? What's he been doing for the last decade and a half? It doesn't make any sense, and, more to the point, it doesn't fit the profile of any serial killer I ever heard of. The vast majority have below-average IQs, are underachievers, and are socially inadequate. Not an ideal profile for a guy who has to persuade half a nation to vote for him."

She pursed her lips into a vast pink haze on the corner of my eye. "Not a known serial killer profile, unless," she said, "you count Hitler and his crowd of crazies as serial killers."

"That is a very unsettling thought, Dehan. I think we need to be searching for a simpler explanation, not a crazier one."

She gave me a big, wet kiss on my cheek, without having to move forward at all, then rolled on her back and closed her eyes.

"*Entia non sunt multiplicanda,*" she said without opening them, "*praeter necesitatem.*"

I turned to stare at her. "What?" But she was already asleep.

ELEVEN

I called Henry on the way back to London the next morning, and he met us in the lobby at the hotel. He looked embarrassed and kept saying, "Right!" like he was gearing himself up to do something. I pointed to a nest of chairs and a sofa in a quiet corner and guided him over. As we sat, he said, "So, do anything nice yesterday? Sorry I didn't call."

Dehan grinned and said, "Yeah, we went down to visit Chiddie and Fi. It was a scream, wasn't it, Stone?"

He laughed like he should know what we were talking about, but didn't. I said, "Lord Chiddester and his wife invited us down to Sussex, for dinner and a chat."

The laughter melted out of his face. "You have to be bloody kidding me. What are you like? How'd you manage that?"

"Maybe I'll tell you later. But first, you have something on your mind, Henry. What is it? Unburden yourself."

He sighed. "I'm getting a bit of flack, to be honest. The people upstairs are asking questions about the direction this case is taking. It started out a clear-cut case of murder, and now suddenly we have senior political figures getting dragged in . . ."

I raised my eyebrows. "We do?"

His look of embarrassment deepened. "Well, Lord Chiddester . . ."

Dehan was frowning. "I'm confused. Isn't he the victim's father? That isn't exactly getting dragged in, Henry. He's not her father because somebody came up with a crazy theory. He's her father because Chiddie and Fi begat Katie."

"Yes, I *know* that, but . . ."

"But all the clues keep leading to politics instead of guys in tinfoil hats."

He sighed again. "Something like that."

Dehan made a face and leaned back in her chair. "You're not wrong . . ." She glanced at me and I nodded. She went on, "Chiddester and his wife believe that Katie was investigating ties between the Labour Party, Marxist groups, and Al-Qaeda cells in London."

He rubbed his face with his hands. "Bloody hell, I was dreading as much."

I said, "It gets worse, Henry."

He looked away and shook his head. "How?"

"She thought the trail led back to a shadow cabinet minister . . . Justin . . . ?"

Dehan said, "Justin Caulfield."

"The shadow foreign secretary."

He had gone the color of wet ash.

I spread my hands. "If she was right, it could be your chance, Henry. Pull it off, close the case, write the book, get rich, and save your marriage."

He showed me a face that said I was out of my mind. "You have to be joking."

"C'mon, Henry! What happened to your killer instinct? If she's right, you have a son of a bitch poised to become foreign secretary, or worse, prime minister; a bastard who is prepared to foster terrorism and murder a young woman to save his own neck. Go get this bastard!"

He sighed. "Do you give credence to it?" He turned to Dehan. "Do you?"

Dehan made a face. "Right now, I don't see any reason not to. Plus . . ." She glanced at me.

I said, "Henry, if you'll forgive me, I think you are looking at this the wrong way. I think you've got so freaked by the political implications that you have stopped looking at the evidence. You are a cop, you are not a politician. Let them worry about the politics. You follow the evidence, wherever it may lead. And you nail the bastard."

"So you do give it credence . . ."

I raised my thumb. "One, it is not the serial killer from fifteen years ago. So stop looking for him. Now follow the evidence. Where does it lead?" I frowned and dropped my hand. "Speaking of which, I didn't hear from the lab. What happened with Johnson's sample? Also the sheets from Katie's apartment and her house."

He took a big breath, then seemed to sag as he let it out. "Okay, the sample you brought us. It's a match for Johnson . . ."

"Stop." I pulled out my phone and emailed the inspector: *DNA under my wife's nails a match for Brad Johnson. Her file attached. Request you back me up on this one, sir. He needs to be tried in Arizona.*

I attached the file Henry's secretary had sent me and sent it to the inspector, back at the 43rd. When I had finished, I said, "Go on."

"There was DNA on the sheets. We haven't found a match yet. But . . ." He sighed again and wouldn't look at us. "I'm sorry, John, Carmen. I feel awful. It was me who asked you to help on this case, and I feel just terrible." Finally he looked at me. "I had to report to my superiors, and to the Crown Prosecution Service, how we came by that sample—the Brad Johnson sample. Of course, the judge will have to rule on its probative value, but however he rules, my DCI . . ."

He paused. I smiled, leaned forward, and slapped him on the

shoulder. "Don't sweat it, Henry. It's me who should be apologizing to you. It was unforgivable of me to behave like that when you had recommended me as a consultant. I will apologize personally to your DCI."

"That's big of you... but..."

"What you're trying to tell us is that he wants us off the case and he'd like us to go back to New York."

He nodded.

"Well, that's not unexpected. Don't feel bad. My behavior was unacceptable, and I am sorry I caused you embarrassment."

He stared at me for a long moment. "That is a very gracious apology, John, but I know what you're saying. You're saying you'd do it all again if you had to."

I nodded. "I got the son of a bitch who killed my wife. And I will have him extradited and I'll see him tried in Arizona."

He went very quiet. Dehan watched him without speaking. Finally, he said, "That's it, isn't it? It's what we both had, but I lost." He turned his head to look at me. "You lost Hattie, and it made you more aggressive, more tenacious, more determined. I kept my wife, had kids, made a family, and that made me more ready to compromise, to keep the status quo, to avoid upsetting the applecart. I was wrong to do that."

I shrugged. "I don't know. I'm not going to tell you what to do, Henry, or how to do it. But if you want my opinion, it's this: if you're going to be a cop, be the best cop you can, and that means you bring down the Archbishop of Canterbury if he breaks the law. If you can't do that, do something else that allows you to be with your wife and kids. But don't hang in the middle."

We stared at each other a moment, then Dehan said, "We done with the life coaching seminar? If we're off the case, you need to know: we talked to Chiddester and his wife about this mysterious Jewish Mr. X that Sadiq was talking about. They have no idea who he is, though Fi was pretty sure that Katie *was* involved with somebody, but she was keeping quiet about who he was."

He nodded. "Thanks . . ." He looked embarrassed again. "Um . . ."

I laughed. "When are we going to leave?"

"Yeah, sorry . . ."

"Well, let us shower, pack, have dinner tonight. Next available flight tomorrow? Will that satisfy your DCI?"

He raised his hands. "Yes, of course, and there is no need to rush. You're not being kicked out or anything like that. It's just . . ."

Dehan leaned forward and slapped him on the shoulder. "Hey! No sweat, Henry. We need to get back anyway. It's been great, but I'm missing the Bronx."

He stood. "Okay, thanks for being understanding. I'll see you before you go . . ."

I said, "Henry?"

"Yeah?"

"I need the DNA report."

He stared at me for a long moment, then reached in his pocket and pulled out his cell. He tapped at his screen a few times and my phone pinged. "That's it now. You're here on holiday, right?"

I gave him the thumbs-up. "You got it, pal."

We watched him walk away, through the exquisite lobby and out into the muggy, midday glare outside.

Dehan crossed her legs and sat tapping her fingers on her knee while I stared absently at the door where moments before, Henry's hazy silhouette had vanished. After a moment, she said, "I guess you were pretty badly out of order."

I nodded. "Mm-hm . . ."

"We'd do the same, if a British cop came over and did that . . ."

I laughed. "Depends. I can think of some PDs where they might offer to hold the suspect down while Inspector Watkins gives him a damned good thrashing, what!"

She laughed at my attempt at an English accent. Then her laugh trailed off. "Still, he was under a lot of pressure . . ."

"Drop it, Dehan. It's not our case. We'll telephone Chiddester and..."

As I was saying it, my phone started to ring. It was a London landline.

"Yeah, Stone."

"Detective John Stone of the NYPD?"

"This is he," I said, rather grandly, and smiled at Dehan.

"I am calling from Justin Caulfield MP's office. He was wondering if you would be kind enough to come in for a chat. We would be happy to send a cab for you."

I drew breath to say that I was afraid we couldn't, but heard my voice saying, "Yeah, sure, but we are on the clock, so it would have to be right now."

"I'll have a taxi pick you up in ten minutes, Detective Stone."

"That'll be fine."

Dehan spread her hands and made a "What?" face.

"Justin Caulfield's office. Would we mind popping in for a chat?"

JUSTIN CAULFIELD'S office was two hundred yards around the corner from where we had seen Lord Chiddester the day before. It was a similar, terraced, Georgian house in dark gray brick with modest white stucco around the door and windows. We were met by a young man in a double-breasted suit who led us up a flight of stairs to a broad landing, where he tapped on a door and then pushed in without waiting for a reply. "Detectives Stone and Dehan, Mr. Caulfield."

He nodded, turned to us, and gestured us in. It was a spacious office, sparsely furnished, and it clearly wasn't his. There was a modest wooden desk beside a closed, white door, a couple of chairs, a bookcase with anonymous volumes on law and parliamentary procedure, and a complete absence of anything personal like photos, paintings, ornaments, or trophies. He stood as we came in and came around the desk to greet us.

He was tall, reedy, with unbrushed short, graying hair. He had a scraggy beard, a tweed jacket, and no tie, but a glance at his shoes told me they cost him at least three hundred bucks. He held out his hand, a man of the people.

"John, Carmen, may I? I am always more comfortable on first-name terms."

Dehan took his hand. "Well, that depends, Mr. Caulfield, on why you invited us here. Why don't you tell us that, and then we'll see about what we call each other."

He threw back his head and laughed loudly. You got the impression he was observing himself doing it and approved of his own bluff, rugged honesty: a man's man who was sensitive enough to be a woman's man too.

He gestured us to the chairs at the desk and spoke as he sat. "One of the things I find so refreshing about America. The directness and the honesty . . ."

I offered him a sweet, honest American smile and said, "That's funny. I was reading in the paper only yesterday that you had had just about enough of our American hypocrisy."

"Taken out of context, I promise."

"I am sure it was. But I am wondering, Mr. Caulfield, what a shadow cabinet minister wants with two cops from the Bronx spending more than they can afford on their honeymoon."

"Congratulations. Even if it is an outmoded institution, it has its romantic charm. But I have to say, that is not an entirely accurate description of your position here at the moment, is it?"

Dehan said, "You're talking about the fact that DI Henry Green asked us to consult on the Katie Ellison murder?"

He nodded.

"How is that any of your business?"

He looked startled.

Dehan spread her hands. "Forgive my direct American honesty, Mr. Caulfield. I don't mean to be rude, I am genuinely asking. If I were back home and a congressman called me into his office to ask about a homicide I was investigating, I'd ask him the same question. What the hell are you doing calling me into your office to ask me about an ongoing investigation?"

He blinked a few times.

I smiled and said, "I was going to ask the same thing, but Detective Dehan is so much more direct and succinct."

He leaned back in his chair and frowned. "And absolutely correct, of course. Which is why I have *not* called you into my main office in the Commons, but rather invited you to this far less formal, *unofficial* office. I certainly did not mean the invitation to be inappropriate in any way."

"That's good to hear. So how can we help you, Mr. Caulfield?"

"Well..." He nodded a few times with his fingers laced across his belly. "There are rumors going around Westminster that the murder of this poor girl might be linked somehow to an MP. If that were the case, clearly there would be a serious national security issue, and I am afraid the government is not always as forthcoming or transparent as it ought to be when it comes to sharing information with the opposition."

Dehan frowned and suddenly grabbed her hair and tied it at the back of her neck, like she was sending it to the naughty mat. "I still don't understand, Mr. Caulfield. I can see that the home secretary, or his aides, might have access to information about an ongoing investigation, but how would you be entitled to that information?"

He blinked again, several times, and almost looked embarrassed. Finally, he said, "If it were a matter of national security, then the shadow home secretary might be entitled to have sight of that information..."

I nodded, frowning like that made sense and putting him at his ease. "I am curious," I said, "as to what makes you think there might be a national security issue in this case."

Now he was on safer ground again. "Well, that is what I was

hoping you would tell me, as everybody else seems to be very tight-lipped about it. All we are getting is rumors that Lord Chiddester's daughter might have been involved with people who *might* have had ties with terrorists."

I frowned deeper, like this was news to me. "May I ask you who suggested that idea to you?"

"I am not at liberty to say."

Dehan laughed and shook her head. "Let me see if I've got this straight. You want us to share confidential information with you about an ongoing investigation, when we are only guests in this country, but you won't tell us the source of your rumors?" She shrugged and spread her hands. "Forgive me but, what's in it for us? Why would we play this game with you?"

He sighed. His face said he was regretting having called us. "Westminster is full of people who share information. Sometimes it's to curry favor, sometimes it's a trade, sometimes it's a sale, for hard cash . . ." He paused, looking first at me and then at Dehan. "And sometimes it is out of loyalty and idealism. Even if I were to give you names, they would mean nothing to you. It is the vine, the bush telegraph of Westminster. All I can tell you is that, if the rumors are true, it would mean a very serious breach of security within the establishment."

I leaned forward and put my elbows on my knees. Then I looked him squarely in the eye. "So you want to know if Katie Ellison was involved with somebody who posed a threat to British national security?"

His breathing quickened barely perceptibly. "Yes . . ."

"We haven't found any indication of that, Mr. Caulfield. But I can tell you that I, personally, know who killed her, and why. And I am closing in on him. So be reassured, there is no threat to your national security, and her killer will soon be behind bars." I glanced at my watch. "I'm afraid we have to go. You take care now."

I stood, and Dehan stood with me. He watched us and his jaw went slack. We crossed the room, gave him a nod, and let ourselves out. I closed the door and his secretary looked up at us and smiled. "Leaving so soon?"

I nodded. "Yeah, you take it easy."

I crossed the floor to the landing, then stopped like I'd forgotten something and crossed back to Caulfield's office. His secretary half stood, looking alarmed. I frowned, shook my head at him, and opened the door.

The white door behind Caulfield's desk was open. Caulfield was standing, staring at me. His expression was one of anger. Opposite him was a slim, dark-haired man of about forty-eight, in a pin-striped suit. I nodded at Caulfield. "Sorry, I thought I forgot my hat, but I didn't bring one."

I closed the door, and Dehan and I made our way down the stairs to the street. Once outside, it was good to feel the river breeze on my face in the muggy heat. Dehan stood, squinting up at me. "What was that about, Sensei? Going back like that?"

I looked up at the low ceiling of gray clouds, then frowned down at her. "I don't know," I said. "I'm not sure."

TWELVE

We were standing in the Victoria Tower Gardens, just beside the Houses of Parliament. We were leaning on the wall, in the shade of the giant chestnut trees, looking out over the Thames. Overhead, the seagulls had stopped laughing at me and instead seemed to be screaming, "*Oh God!*" to the heavens in their ugly, squawking voices.

"I noticed the door," I said to Dehan. "The whole office was obviously improvised. That whole area: Little College Street, Great College Street, Cowley, Barton, they're all given over to the use of backbench MPs, to run campaigns, meet delegations . . ."

She was nodding. "A spillover from the main government offices in the Houses of Parliament."

"Exactly. He wanted to meet us unofficially, so it made sense to use an office one of his minions was probably using for something else. But it struck me when we went in that it was an odd place to have the desk. It was kind of awkward, right by a door, when it would have made more sense to have it closer to a window." I spread my hands. "Better light, nice view . . . It just kept nagging at me, and in the end I decided he had somebody on the other side of the door, listening."

"And that's why you went back? To see who it was?"

I nodded out at the river. A barge hooted at me.

"So who was it?"

I didn't answer. I couldn't answer. Finally, she asked me, "Are you going to answer?"

I sighed. "I don't know how to. I have no idea who it was. It was a man in a charcoal-gray, pin-striped, single-breasted three-piece suit. It was a nice suit, well cut, understated. Other than that, he was nondescript: dark hair, medium build, five eleven, maybe six foot."

I frowned at myself because I knew there was more to it than that, but I wasn't sure what. Dehan managed to frown and raise an eyebrow at the same time, which takes skill. "You seem to have noticed his suit more than him."

She was right, and I nodded a lot. "Yes, because somehow, Dehan, and this is going to sound crazy, but somehow, the suit was more important than he was."

She made a face and shrugged. "No, yeah, I can see how you would think that sounds crazy. That's because it is crazy, Stone!" She turned to face me and slapped me gently across the back of my head. "How can the guy's suit be more important than he is? Come on! I gotta get you home before you start turning as crazy as these Brits! I think you're reverting to your ancestral madness!"

I laughed. She took my left arm in both of hers and started walking me back toward Abingdon Street. "Now, there are two places you are going to take me, which I heard are 'must-sees' in London. One is a pub that used to be the Bank of England. You got to hand it to these people, they know what to do with an old building. Turn it into a pub. That is genius. The second is an ancient bar called El Vino."

I nodded as I pulled my cell from my pocket. "I know both of those places very well. They are both on the same street. Just give me a second."

I made a call while Dehan hailed a cab. It answered on the third ring. A black cab pulled over, and as we climbed in, I said into the phone, "Manuel, I am going to email you a file. Can you print it for me and have it ready for when I arrive back, in an hour or two? Keep it in the safe till we get in, will you? Thanks."

The cab did a U-turn and we headed east toward Parliament Square. I leaned forward and said, "Can you drop us at the Temple Gardens? We'll walk from there."

"Lovely walk," he said, and didn't stop talking till we got there. By the time he dropped us off and I'd paid him, we knew all about his missus, where his kids went to school, why the country was going to the dogs, and how immigration had brought the country to its knees. I figured that was one vote for Chiddester.

We walked through the Temple Gardens gate and up Middle Temple Lane. For my money, it is one of the most bizarre and lovely places on the planet. The roads are cobbled; every building is between three and five hundred years old and still inhabited by lawyers who wear black gowns and wigs. We walked among the colonnades and flagged paths, through Pump Court, and came out at the Inner Temple, with the great dining hall on the right, beside the library, and the Temple, the ancient church itself, on the left.

I pointed to it. "The Magna Carta had its first reading right in there. It was a Templar church back then. An Englishman's right to trial by jury, his right to legal representation, all date back to this place in the twelfth and thirteenth century." I smiled at her. "You're looking at the taproot of our own constitution, Dehan. The rule of law, an equitable legal system, innocence till proven guilty, it all starts right here."

She leaned her head on my shoulder. "So when we have a son of a bitch in custody and he lawyers up . . ."

I ignored her. "Thomas Heyward, Thomas Lynch, Edward Rutledge . . . There are over a dozen signatories of the Declaration of Independence and the Constitution who were members of either the Inner Temple or the Middle Temple, who learned their law right here."

As I said it, I thought of Brad Johnson, lying on the floor of his apartment, with his bloodied face and his broken leg. The rule of law, innocent till proved guilty . . . until it's your own wife or your own child. Suddenly, I felt oddly uncomfortable among those ancient buildings; suddenly, they seemed to be glaring at me, like the vengeful ghosts of ancient jurists. I put my arm around her and moved toward Dr Johnson's Buildings.

"C'mon, Dehan," I said. "Let's get some lunch at the Bank."

Dr Johnson's Buildings is a narrow, flagged alley that leads to an ancient Tudor gate onto Fleet Street. Directly opposite is Chancery Lane, and slightly to the left of that is the Old Bank of England, vast, elaborately elegant in eighteenth-century style and packed to the gunnels with noise lawyers holding pints of beer and glasses of wine.

We elbowed our way through the crowds to one of the alcoves at the back where they had tables set for lunch. We had two pints of bitter and two steak and kidney pies, and pretended to ignore the Katie Ellison case. Just once, Dehan, with her mouth full of pie and a second pint of bitter in her hand, said, "Tho, wha' chou hab de 'oncierge primp?"

"What did I have the concierge print?"

She nodded.

"The original Butcher file."

She swallowed. "Why?"

I shrugged. "For my records."

"You can't print it for your phony, nonexistent records back in New York? We have to carry a ton of paper in our luggage instead? You're lying. Remember, the penalty for cutting me out is . . ."

"Okay, don't threaten me on a full stomach. I want to see why that suit is so important."

"You're out of your mind. You, John Stone . . ." She pointed at me with her fork. "Are officially insane."

A girl in a French maid's uniform came to take our plates and I asked her for two Bushmills and some Stilton cheese. She said prettily that she would bring that for me right away and vanished.

Dehan drained her glass and tried unsuccessfully not to belch.

"It's moments like these," I said, "I am reminded why I married you."

"Seriously, Stone, A: how are you going to see why a suit is important by going through a fifteen-year-old case file; B: how can a three-piece pin-striped suit be remotely relevant to anything; and C: we are off the case and going home to the 'Bwonx' tomorrow. You solved your wife's murder. Let it go."

"A: I don't know; B: I don't know; and C: okay."

We had our whiskey and Stilton and, feeling slightly overfed, stepped out into the early-afternoon heat. The clouds had largely cleared overhead and, though the humidity had lessened, it was still in the high nineties. We decided to give El Vino a miss and instead turned up Chancery Lane, intending to get the metro—or the Underground—to Piccadilly and crash for an hour or two in our suite before packing in the afternoon.

On the way up, we passed Ede & Ravenscroft, the oldest tailor in London. Dehan guided me toward the large, dark wood window display and said, "1689, that's a good run for any business. That the kind of suit your guy was wearing?"

It was. It was exactly the kind of suit he was wearing. And it was as though she had dropped a pinch of yeast into my brain and it had started fermenting. I nodded. "Exactly. It's important, Dehan. It's the missing link we have been looking for, and I can't think why. What the hell does it mean?"

She frowned up at me. "You're serious, aren't you?"

"Yeah . . ." I pointed through the glass at the dummy: his crisp white shirt, the collar held on with studs, the charcoal-gray, single-breasted jacket, waistcoat and pants, the high-gloss black shoes. It was the key, and somewhere inside my brain I knew why, but it wouldn't come to me. Every time I tried to grasp it, it dissipated, like charcoal-gray mist. "That suit, right there. That is the answer."

She shook her head. "I don't see it, Sensei."

"Neither do I, Little Grasshopper. In this case, Sensei trury brind."

She grabbed my arm and pulled me away. "Come on! I am sleepy. Let's get a cab. I don't feel like traveling in a tube today."

At the hotel, Manuel collected the printed file for me and we went up to our suite. There we showered and Dehan fell onto the bed and went immediately to sleep. I sat by the open window and worked my way steadily through the old file. Much of it I remembered—at least the broad strokes, the overall shape, the main characters and players. But there were also many details I had forgotten. I had blurred in my mind how central Brad Johnson had been to the case. I remembered as I read how blinded Henry and his colleagues had become by Johnson. They were certain he was their man, and I knew for a fact that he wasn't.

Then everything had happened at once. Hattie had been killed. I had gone to pieces. Inexplicably, the Crown Prosecution Service had dropped Johnson overnight as their prime suspect in the Butcher investigation. I had been shipped back to the States and the whole thing had gone cold.

I had never understood why the CPS dropped Johnson, but Henry and I had lost touch, and I guess, as I had never believed he was guilty of those particular murders, I never saw the point in looking into it.

But now I wondered. Now it began to nag at the back of my mind, along with the pin-striped suit: the kind of suits that the CPS wear. In fact, Ede & Ravenscroft were exactly that, tailors to the Bar. That was their specialization. They made suits for barristers.

So where did that get me? I heaved a sigh, stood, and paced about for a bit. Nowhere. It got me exactly nowhere. I went and stood looking out of the window at Green Park. A suit. A pin-striped suit.

Then I had a thought. Fifteen years earlier, cooperation between British and American law enforcement was in its infancy. That was one reason why I had been there in the first place, and I had often thought since that there was something I should have done—we should have done—which we never did. Partly because to begin with, the team was so sure it was Johnson, and then because I had left and the case had gone cold.

I pulled out my cell and called Bernie at the bureau. We had been friends for over ten years and he had often helped out when I needed to cut through red tape.

"Stone, you back already? How was it? You divorced yet?"

I laughed. "Almost. Actually, I'm still here. Listen, I've been meaning to ask you this for about fifteen years."

"I didn't think we knew each other that long. Either way, Stone, I'm straight, and even if I wasn't, I am scared of your wife."

"Shut up, Bernie, and listen. Going back from 2003, a serial killer, uncaught, anywhere in the States, trademarks are as follows: victims of choice are young women, blond, roughly five-five to five-eight, probably nurses. He rapes them, stabs them in the heart with a kitchen knife, cuts out their wombs postmortem, and then—and this is crucial—he blinds them, pins a note to their left eye with a meat skewer. The note is inscribed with a line from Don McLean's song 'American Pie,' 'And them good ole boys were drinking whisky and rye . . .' ending on a dot dot dot."

He was silent for a moment and you could almost hear him thinking. "You know, I want to say that nothing springs to mind, and nothing does in terms of a name or anything, but it does sound kind of familiar."

"You may be thinking of the British Butcher of Whitechapel case."

"No, if I'm not making it up, this is one of those Midwest cases, or Deep South. You know, those places where everybody suffers from narrow head syndrome and Seth's daddy is also his brother *and* his son."

"That's impossible."

"But you get the idea."

"I do. Will you have a look? There is a U.S. angle to this case which we never properly explored back in the day. And it's resurfaced now."

"Sure. If there is anything, it shouldn't be hard to find with these details."

"Appreciate it, Bernie."

I hung up. I paced a bit more. I sat down again, talking to myself in my head. *So, assume, for argument's sake, that there was a guy, an American, in what Bernie would call Narrow Heads Ville. He is deeply disturbed and starts killing women in this ritualistic fashion. For some reason which is hard to fathom, he moves to the U.K., to London, and continues his killing spree. We investigate. Henry and his team fixate on Johnson. Johnson kills my wife to scare me off, I go home. And at some point during that period, Narrow Head Man suddenly and permanently stops killing. Maybe he died. Maybe he was miraculously cured.*

But, fifteen years later, somebody kills Katie Ellison. The choice of victim is not part of a serial killer's victim profile. The choice of victim is deliberate. But the killer imitates Narrow Head Man perfectly, in every detail, except that the victim is not a one hundred percent perfect match for Narrow Head Man's victim of choice, she is a little shorter, and she is English, not American. The spelling of whiskey is also English, not American...

Where the Butcher of Whitechapel had been an American case, Katie Ellison was an English case.

It was as though the darkness in my mind slowly began to crack. Slivers of light began to filter through, things began to connect, link up, and make sense. I reached for the file and began to leaf through it furiously, searching for a reference, and finally, there, on the third from last page, I saw it. And the memory flooded back. I sank slowly into my chair. I had it. I had the missing link. And it was a pin-striped suit.

THIRTEEN

THE PROBLEM WAS HOW TO PROVE IT. I SPENT HALF AN hour staring unseeing at the sky through the window and finally, I picked up my phone and called Henry.

"John, we haven't sorted your ticket yet, but I've got the lad on it now."

"Henry, why did the team drop the investigation against Brad Johnson?"

"John! Come on, mate!"

"Humor me, I am just curious. You were all crazy about him and then overnight, you dropped him as your prime suspect."

"Um . . ." He paused and sighed. "It's there in the file . . ."

"All it says is 'acting on advice from the CPS.'"

He thought for a minute. "Yeah, they said they had received information and that they were satisfied Johnson was not guilty of the murders and that on advice from the home secretary, they were recommending that the case should not be investigated further."

"Did that strike you as odd?"

"Yes, of course it did. And doubly odd when he showed up again and then Katie Ellison died. But if we were told not to go after Johnson, and we had bugger all else to go on, *and* the home secretary is telling us to drop it, what could we do? *And* the killing stopped, so there were no fresh leads. Look, can't you just let it rest, John? Look, I'll have the tickets couriered to you in the next hour, okay?"

"Sure. Thanks, Henry."

I dialed again.

"Chiddester!"

"Good afternoon, Chiddester, it's Stone here. I may have some information of use to you."

"Really? What?"

"I need access to a file. In 2003, the Crown Prosecution Service advised the Serious Crimes squad that Brad Johnson, their prime suspect, was not guilty of the Butcher of Whitechapel murders. No explanation. The home secretary then recommended that investigation of the case should cease. After that, there were no more murders. I am satisfied that I know almost everything that happened, and I know who killed Katie, but I can't prove it. If I can see that file, I might just be able to bring it home."

He was quiet for a long moment, then said, "Leave it with me."

He hung up and I paced for half an hour, achieving nothing but a slight flattening of my path on the rug. Then the phone rang. I was surprised to see it was Bernie.

"That wasn't difficult, Stone. Popped up straightaway, but it was never solved."

"I know."

"Course you do. You know everything. Westminster, Colorado. Three girls killed over a three-year period. Susie..."

"Don't give me the names, I won't remember. Can you outline the basic facts and then email me the file?"

"Whatever. The girls were killed like you described them, with the note pinned to the eye like you said..." He paused, like he was trying to multitask. "File's on its way. Yeah, with the line from 'American Pie.' They were all nurses, or involved in caring for people. The sheriff was pretty sure he knew who the killer was, but before he could arrest him, he took off and disappeared."

"Who did he suspect?"

"Simon Clarence."

I frowned. "Simon Clarence? Doesn't sound . . ."

"I know. But his mom was local, his dad wasn't. His dad was from Barbados. Seems Mom was a couple of cans short of a six-pack, and Dad liked to use his belt, on the whole family, not just the kids. Violent man, rap sheet for assault, use of a deadly weapon . . ."

"I get the idea. He was cruel to the wife and the kids."

"Yup, sheriff tried to intervene a few times, but they all told him to take a hike. Mom died in suspicious circumstances when Simon was ten, probably witnessed it, if you ask me. Not much more to tell. They were kind of travelers, neo-hippies, moved around a bit. Simon was born in the U.K. . . ."

"So he had dual nationality?"

"Yup. Dad was a British citizen; Simon was born in the U.K. and they came back to the States when he was just two, settled in Colorado."

"And he disappeared, what, 2002, 2003?"

"2002. So did he show up in the U.K.?"

"He showed up in London, killed four women, and then vanished off the face of the Earth."

"Maybe he's in Barbados."

"Yeah, maybe. But I don't think so."

"You going to let me in?"

"Not yet, but soon. Thanks, Bernie, I owe you."

"I lost count how much you owe me. If I ever call it in, I'll die of alcohol poisoning."

We promised to catch up soon and I hung up. Dehan appeared in the bedroom doorway and looked at me with sleepy eyes behind lots of hair. She shook her head at me and went away to the shower. Then the phone rang again.

"Stone, Chiddester here. It's not much help, I'm afraid. Fine work on your part, but . . ."

"Simon Clarence approached the Crown Prosecution Service through defense counsel . . . ?"

He was silent. Then, "How could you possibly have known that?"

"Ah, you know, eliminate the impossible . . . So what have you got?"

"Well, I didn't know his name. The file is sealed, and there is only a very brief abstract available. It seems this, um, Clarence had started to see a psychiatrist. The psychiatrist was so disturbed by what he learnt, and by what he was reading in the press, putting two and two together, as it were, that he felt he had no choice but to violate patient confidentiality. However, rather than go to the police, being a somewhat eminent fellow with some pull in the establishment, he arranged a series of meetings with a judge and the director of public prosecutions, and sectioned the chap, to be detained at Her Majesty's leisure at Goodnestone Park."

"What is that, a high-security mental institution?"

"Precisely."

I shook my head. "That's not the full picture, Chiddester. There was somebody else involved. Let me see if I'm right. Either his psychiatrist arranged, or the judge appointed, but at some point during the proceedings Simon Clarence was given counsel."

"Oh, yes, naturally."

"Does the counsel's name appear on the abstract?"

"Of course."

"Can you send me a scan of that abstract? Once I have read it, I can give you the name of the man who killed your daughter."

"Good Lord! You mean it wasn't Sadiq?"

"I told you it wasn't."

He grunted. "All right, the scan is on its way. But I'll need convincing, Stone. My money is still on Sadiq Hassan."

"Okay, just don't do anything rash. Listen, I need one more favor from you."

"It's you who are doing me a favor, dear boy. If I can help, I will."

"I need to visit Clarence at Goodnestone, either as a friend of the family or as American cops clearing up unsolved American murders. Whatever you think will work. Can you pull strings?"

"I'll see what I can do."

He hung up. My phone pinged to tell me an email had arrived, and I opened it and read it. It told me exactly what I expected it to tell me. So I went to the bathroom, where Dehan was looking at herself in a large mirror, wet and wrapped in many white towels. "I found the Butcher of Whitechapel."

She glanced at me in the mirror. "Okay, what's the punch line?"

I shook my head. "No punch line. His name is Simon Clarence. He's in a high-security mental institution called Goodnestone Park. He's been there since 2003."

She turned to stare at me from among her towels. "Are you kidding me? How come Henry didn't know?"

"It was kept quiet because the way it was handled, though probably wise, might have caused a public outcry. The file was sealed, and his identity was not revealed. He was sectioned, and the home secretary instructed the police to stand down on the investigation."

"I lie down for a siesta and you solve world hunger. How?"

"It was the suit."

"Oh, yeah, right. I see that now."

"I'll explain properly in the car."

"Oh, the car, right... What car?"

"We are going to visit Simon Clarence in Goodnestone Park."

She sighed. "Does Henry know?"

I mouthed something obscene at her.

She laughed and turned back to the mirror. "Well, that's true. So what about Katie? How does she tie in to all this?"

"We may never know," I said vaguely as I thumbed a text

message on my phone. "On the other hand, we may find out tonight."

The phone rang as I pressed Send.

"Stone."

"Chiddester here. I pulled some strings and they're expecting your visit at six. I said it was an unofficial fact-finding mission sanctioned by the Home Office to help families in the States find some closure. I believe that's the popular term. Anyway, I thought that would give you maximum elbow room."

"That's perfect."

He hesitated. "Have you got a name yet?"

"Yes. But let me prove it, Chiddester. It isn't straightforward. It's complicated. But I hope to have the whole thing wrapped up by tomorrow morning, at the latest."

He gave a reluctant grunt. "Very well."

"I'll keep you posted, I promise."

I called down to reception for them to arrange me a car, and twenty minutes later, after I had showered and we had both dressed, we went downstairs. I signed for the vehicle, saw the price, thanked the gods in Valhalla that I wasn't paying, and we headed out toward Kent, and the village of Goodnestone.

It was a nice drive. Kent is known as the garden of England, and as we drove down the A2, the countryside all around us was green and abundant, with hedgerows like huge billows of green smoke, heavy and dense, clinging to the hillsides. At Barham, we turned north and east, down small, winding roads and through woodlands, ever deeper into Tolkien landscapes where tall, redbrick chimney pots peered out from among bushy clusters of foliage in every imaginable shade of green. There were villages of just a handful of houses, that had names like Nonington, Easole —which made Dehan giggle like a schoolchild—and Womenswold, which made me think of a department store in Stepford.

Finally, we came to a small crossroads with wooden signs pointing, amusingly, to Ham one way and Sandwich another, and a third pointed to Goodnestone. We followed this road through dense forest, over blacktop dappled with patches of sunlight and the shadows of twisted branches and dancing leaves, until at last we came out of the woods onto the rim of a shallow valley. We stopped a moment to have a look.

Ahead of us, the road, like a thin, black ribbon, curved gently to the east, leading to a small hamlet of ancient, redbrick houses. From there, the road turned sharply west to what looked like an old Georgian manor house, surrounded by smaller, more modern buildings, and several acres of parkland contained within a high wall. This was the Goodnestone High Security Psychiatric Facility, otherwise known as Goodnestone Park.

"It just blows my mind, Stone, that after all these years, it turns out they had him all the time, and never let on. Why would they do that?"

"Politics," I said, then looked at her. "Politics with a small *p*. Not party politics, conservatives, liberals, all that crap. Just avoiding a public outcry. The fewer people who knew about it, the fewer could get upset." I started up the engine again. "When you think about it, it's pretty controversial, with the potential to upset just about everybody. Man gets sentenced to life, without even trial; or, man murders seven women and gets *off* without even a trial. But from a pragmatic point of view, it saved the country a very expensive trial and took a very dangerous man off the streets without the risk of a clever defense counsel getting him off. The file was sealed to protect his identity, which some would also think controversial."

Dehan nodded. "We have a right to know who killed our daughter. I get that."

"Yeah. It's tricky."

I pulled up at the gate and a guy in a private security uniform came over to look in the window. I showed him my driver's license.

"Detectives Stone and Dehan. Lord Chiddester arranged the visit. I believe you are expecting us."

He checked my license and nodded. "Very good, sir. Leave the car in the car park at the right of the main building and report to reception, through the main door."

"Thanks."

We did as he said and ten minutes later pushed into what would originally have been the entrance hall of the manor, but was now a quiet, still reception, paneled in dark wood with bare, highly polished boards on the floor. To our left, there was a woman sitting behind a functional, white counter, looking at us through glasses that reflected the windows and concealed her eyes. Standing, leaning on the counter, smiling at us, was a man in chinos and a white coat, with reading glasses hanging around his neck. He was a well-preserved sixty and knew it. He approached us with his hand held out to Dehan.

"Detectives Dehan and Stone, I believe. I am Dr. Fenshaw, the director of this facility. Shall we go to my office? And you can tell me exactly what it is you want."

We shook his hand and followed him down a short passage to an office with a large window overlooking a lawn at the back of the house. The office was old-world but functional, with leather furniture side by side with sage-green, steel filing cabinets that looked like they had been salvaged from World War I. He waved us to a couple of chairs as he moved behind the desk and we all sat.

"You want to talk to Simon Clarence."

It was more a statement than a question, and it felt like a subtle challenge. I gave him the dead eye and said, "That's why we're here. I hope you didn't have us drive down from London just to tell us we can't see him."

He smiled. "Not at all. Lord Chiddester outlined the reason for your visit and I was happy to help. I am just curious about a couple of points."

"Like how we knew he was here?"

He nodded. "The file is sealed."

"I worked the original murders fifteen years ago. I went back to the States and, almost simultaneously, your investigation here stopped. A recent murder, which has not yet been reported in the press, resurrected that investigation. So I did what I should have done fifteen years ago: I looked to see if there had been similar murders in the States. There had, and the sheriff was pretty sure it was Clarence. So then I looked into why the investigation had stopped. The answer seemed to be, 'We were told to.' After that, with Lord Chiddester's help, it wasn't difficult to get the abstract from the sealed file."

"I see. That makes perfect sense." He gave a small sigh. "Be prepared. Simon is more or less coherent most of the time. He has made some progress over the years, he is . . ." He frowned at his desk like he felt there was something wrong with it, but he wasn't sure what. "He is *attempting* to feel remorse for what he did, but he doesn't know how to. He is a deeply troubled man, who suffered a great deal as a child." He frowned at us. "You may ask him about one thing, and he will answer something that to you may seem completely unrelated and irrelevant, but to him it will make perfect sense. This is to be expected in schizophrenics. I don't know if you will find what you came looking for, but I hope you do."

"Thank you. We'll bear it in mind, but it's pretty much what we expected." I hesitated a moment, then asked, "Doctor, were you his psychiatrist? Was it you who made the move to have him sectioned?"

He studied me for a moment. "Detective, I authorized this visit on the strict understanding that the secret nature of the file would be respected absolutely. Anything I tell you remains strictly between we three."

Chiddester hadn't told me that, but I saw no point arguing, so I said, "That is understood, Doctor."

He nodded a few times, then seemed to examine Dehan's face. "Yes, I was his psychiatrist. I don't know if you realize this, but it is extremely unusual for a schizophrenic to seek the help of a professional. So when Simon came to me, I at first thought that he was simply fantasizing. He had seen the murders in the papers, or on television, and projected himself into them, to make himself feel important. But with the last murder . . ." He gazed away to his left, trying to remember the name.

I said, "Kathleen Dodge."

"Kathleen, Kathleen Dodge, he told me about her before the police found the body. The whole thing was plagued with problems: confidentiality, his status—was he fit to stand trial—witnesses; I would be the only witness and my testimony might be ruled as hearsay . . ." He shook his head. "And then there was the issue of trust. If I reported him to the police, he would feel betrayed, and the only person in the world who had access to him, me, would be lost, he would never talk to me again. It seemed to me that the most sensible thing to do was to have him quietly sectioned, a procedure I was able to make him understand was for his own good."

He made to stand and said, "Why don't I take you to him? I assure you he is medicated and he is not dangerous. Talk to him for a while, see what you get, and then come and see me again."

"Yeah." I nodded. "That's good. Thank you."

And we rose and went to see Simon Clarence.

FOURTEEN

HE WAS SITTING AT A TABLE ON A STONE TERRACE AT the back of the house. A broad lawn swept away toward hedgerows, about a quarter of a mile away, and people, some of them in brilliant white coats and dresses, wandered this way and that, or just sat and stared.

Simon Clarence was dressed in white: white deck shoes, white pants, and a white shirt. He looked up at us as we came out. He was thin, with immensely long limbs, and seated in the chair, he reminded me of a bent wire hanger. I figured he must be at least six foot six, with a large, bony face, high cheekbones, and a strong nose. He could have been good-looking, but there was something unsettling about his stare, like his eyes were searching for something, and didn't care what they had to do to find it.

Fenshaw pulled up a chair and sat opposite him. Then he smiled at us and said, "Sit, sit. This is Simon. Simon, these are some friends of mine who have come to visit you. They have some questions they would like to ask you. I told them you'd be happy to help them. Remember we talked about how good it is to help people?"

He nodded. After what Bernie had told me, I had expected a

dull, simple voice. The voice of a stereotypic inbred. Instead, when he spoke, his voice was clear and articulate.

"Yes, I remember that. I'll try to be helpful, Doctor."

Fenshaw patted him on the arm. "Good man. Give me a shout if you need anything."

He got up and left. Simon watched him go and then looked at us in turn with oddly incurious eyes. His voice had a hint of an American accent, but not much.

"Are you cops? You look like cops from the U.S.A."

Dehan answered, "Yup. We came over from New York, but it's the sheriff of Washington County who asked us to come and see you."

"I don't really understand why they're mad at me. For leaving. They didn't like me there."

Dehan frowned. "What makes you think that?"

"Samuel."

"Samuel?"

"Samuel makes me think that."

"Who is Samuel?"

"Samuel is dead. He was married to my mother. She said he was my daddy. But I'm not sure. He might have been. Sometimes he is. But toward the end, he wasn't." He frowned. "I'm still trying to sort that one out. Dr. Fenshaw is helping me on that one."

I said, "What about the girls?"

He took a deep breath and shifted in his chair. "I am really trying to be cooperative with Dr. Fenshaw on that one too. But, thing is, I don't know if anybody understands me, that there weren't no girls." He gazed out at the green lawn with the white figures. "Things happen that only I understand. I think that's the same for everybody, but not everybody realizes it. That's what makes me special."

"There were no girls?"

"Everybody else thought there were. That's the way they saw it. But when I was doing it . . ." He stared at me a moment, like he wasn't sure if I knew what "doing it" was. He glanced at Dehan. "You know, when I was helping her to understand, and get away from Samuel? There were no girls then. It was just me and Mom, and she was so relieved that I could help her."

"I bet she was."

"She told me she was. But then the problem came up with the girls. Seems every time I helped her, one of them girls got hurt. I don't know how that happened. And it was the same in London, so there was something going on. I'm trying to help Dr. Fenshaw figure it out. That's why I asked Dr. Fenshaw to help me."

Dehan said, "I guess your mom was a nurse."

"Of course. That's why it was always nurses. It goes back to them. Or I couldn't have helped her. She never was able to help me. When Samuel came for us, in the dark, she could never help me. But I was able to help her. With my mind. I have a special mind. That was how I discovered the doors."

I raised an eyebrow. "The Doors or Don McLean?"

He stared at me, blinking. Then he laughed. "You don't understand. The doors in my mind. If I go through the doors, I can go to other places, and other people. So when he was hurting her, I could go through the door in my mind, and go inside her and stop the pain. Stop her from hurting. There were steps you have to follow. The most important one is to still the heart until he's finished. But she could never help me to still my heart. Only I can do that. That's why I had to go away. Cause nobody liked me doing that."

"What about Don McLean?"

"That's Samuel. He goes away and he comes back singing. That's how you know he's going to hurt you. He goes to see the boys, drinking whiskey and rye, and then he comes back singing, 'this'll be the day that you die.' That's when I have to go through the doors. I don't like talking about this."

I glanced at Dehan, thinking I had seen all I needed to see, but before I could stand up, he started talking again.

"I had a sneaky way of getting out through the doors before

he started hitting me. The belt was no good for me. He said that. It didn't make me cry. That was because I'd gone through the door. So he used the buckle, 'cause that didn't make me cry but it made Simon bleed.

"And while he was giving Simon the buckle, I could sneak through the door and go to help Mom. 'Cause she was always right there, on the floor. And I'd get to her before he did, through the door to get inside her and help her. Then he'd put his thing in her, but he said that was dangerous because it might make another little shit like Simon. So when he was finished, he would do things to stop that happening, like punch her. That's why I had to take out her womb. Only till he'd finished beating her. First you still the heart, then you stop the seeing, by making the eyes dark, then take out the womb, so there are no more shits like Simon. Then you bring her to understanding, that it's the song that's warning her. When she hears the song, she has to do something to protect Simon. But it never works. It's always a girl that gets hurt. That's why I asked Dr. Fenshaw to help. I think he's helping, but we're still working on that one."

I nodded. The shadows were growing long across the lawns. Up on the chimney, a blackbird had started its long evening song. I wondered if it was the same one, following me around Britain. I said, "I'm sure he is, Simon. I'm sure things are getting better. Do you get many visitors?"

"No, never. Except the man, once. But I'm not allowed to talk about that."

"The man? You mean Samuel?"

"No. Samuel is dead. Dr. Fenshaw told me Samuel is dead. The man was from the government. He told me I mustn't ever talk about him, or what we discussed."

I smiled, then gave a small laugh. "I bet that surprised you, right?"

He nodded cautiously.

I went on, "Not just getting the visit, which was unexpected, but that he should ask you all the same questions as Dr. Fenshaw, and then tell you it's secret! Right? That doesn't make much sense, does it?"

He shook his head. "Didn't make no sense to me. But Dr. Fenshaw said it was okay."

"Can you remember his name?"

"Peters. Dr. Peters."

"Okay, Simon, thank you very much. You have been very helpful to us. One last question before we leave you in peace. If I show you a photograph of Dr. Peters, would you recognize him?"

"Of course."

I pulled out my wallet and saw Dehan frowning at me. I pulled out the photograph I'd had printed at the hotel and showed it to Simon. He nodded. "Yeah, that's Dr. Peters. I don't know why he said the things he did."

"Well, Simon. Sometimes people are too careful, but I can tell you that you no longer have to keep that a secret. You can tell anybody you like. I'm sure Dr. Fenshaw will say the same thing. You never told him about Dr. Peters' secret questions, did you?"

He shook his head. "He told me not to."

"That's right." I looked at Dehan. She shook her head that she had no questions—not for Simon at least—and we stood. "Take it easy, Simon." I patted his shoulder and we went inside to look for Dr. Fenshaw.

We found him in his office, sitting behind his desk reading a file. He looked up and smiled. "Come in. Sit down. Was the interview helpful?"

We sat, and while I scratched my chin, Dehan asked what I was about to ask. "Who is Dr. Peters?"

He frowned. "I don't know any Dr. Peters."

I said, "Let me ask you a different question. Who was Simon's visitor?"

He went very still. "I am not in a position to answer that question."

I grunted. "That's what I thought you'd say." I put the photograph on the desk and watched his face. "That's him, right? It's okay, Simon already identified him, but he identified him as Dr. Peters. Can you think why he would use a false name to talk to Simon?"

His expression became abstracted. He shook his head slowly, then blinked and shook it more vigorously. "I . . . Really, I am not in a position to answer that question. *Especially* as you have no jurisdiction in this country. Have an English detective come, with a warrant, and I will happily answer any questions you like."

"I understand. Just answer me this, which I am pretty sure is not covered by any kind of privilege. It *should* be a matter of public record, and I am pretty sure you don't want a lot of cops, American or English, tramping around asking this kind of question—was he appointed by the court, did you choose him, or did he offer himself?"

He sighed heavily. "I certainly didn't choose him. As to whether he was appointed by the judge or offered his services, I don't know. It may have been a bit of both. It made sense, anyway, for obvious reasons."

"Okay, thank you, Doctor. I imagine Detective Inspector Green will be in touch in due course. You have been very helpful."

His face didn't really reveal whether he was happy about that or not, probably because he himself wasn't sure.

We stepped out into the evening sunshine and made our way to the car in the small parking lot at the side of the clinic. We pulled out and headed back out the gate, past the small hamlet of Goodnestone and up the long, narrow road through the fields, toward the dark mass of the forest. We had the windows down to let in the warm, evening breeze, and a vast murmuration of starlings swarmed across the sky in the east, seeming to fold over itself and re-form like a bizarre piece of giant, flying plasma. Eventually, it seemed to be sucked into the trees and vanished.

Dehan watched it disappear and spoke, still staring at the trees. "I have to tell you, Stone, I am feeling a little lost here. Who the hell is Dr. Peters now?"

We were swallowed by the trees and engulfed suddenly in

green-mottled darkness. The headlamps came on and we plunged ever deeper into a long, black tunnel, split here and there by thin slashes of evening sunlight. I glanced in the mirror and saw the glowing portal of light through which we had entered diminishing and withdrawing behind us.

"Dr. Peters was a fake name," I said.

She looked at me with a face of irony. "Yeah, I'd got that far, Sherlock. I'm asking who he is in reality. Who is the guy in the photograph?"

"Well, I still have to prove the connection, Dehan. But the guy in the photograph was Brad Johnson's defense attorney back in 2003. It looks like he was appointed to represent Simon Clarence when Dr. Fenshaw decided to section him . . ."

Her eyebrows shot up. "Holy attorneys, Batman . . ."

"Have you got your seat belt on?"

"Of course, why?"

"Things could get bumpy."

I was watching the mirror, and a car had just pulled out from a narrow, overgrown path behind us and was closing fast. I began to accelerate, speeding toward the glowing end of the long tunnel of trees. The car behind us switched on its headlamps and continued to close, gaining speed. Then it was pulling over to the right-hand side of the road, aiming to overtake. I heard a roar of a powerful engine and what I could now see was a dark blue Audi drew level with us. I glanced and saw an extended arm and the glint of metal. I bellowed, "*Brace!*" and slammed on the brakes.

Dehan lunged forward, covering her head with her arms. The Audi overshot us and I saw a flash of flame inside the cab. Hot rage welled up in my belly. I let out the clutch, floored the gas, and climbed through the gears, first, second, third, fourth, until I was inches from his trunk. Then I floored the clutch and the gas at the same time. The revs screamed into the red and at six thousand revs, I released the clutch. We were maybe three feet from the Audi. The engine bit, the car bucked, and we surged forward, smashing hard into the Audi's trunk. As the steel bit, I yanked the steering wheel right, dragging his rear axle with me into the middle of the road.

Then I braked steadily, keeping control as he skidded sideways away from me down the blacktop. I growled at Dehan, "Stay down!"

Then I floored the gas again, charging straight for his passenger door. I could see a cowering silhouette inside, covering its head with its arms. I muttered something unprintable about trying to shoot my wife and reached for the handbrake. Then shouted something equally unprintable about the jackasses who decided to replace the handbrake with a stupid button. I spun the wheel hard left and hit the brake pedal.

It wasn't exactly a handbrake turn, but the car swung its ass in a big arc and smashed hard into the side of the Audi, lifting it onto two wheels and rolling it twice over to the side of the road, where it came to rest on its roof against a tree.

Dehan came out of her brace position and stared at me. "*Jesus*, Stone!"

I put it into first, then second, and gently rolled over to where the Audi was lying, belly-up, with its wheels still spinning. I grinned at her. "You like that?"

I climbed out. His automatic was lying on the road, thirty feet back. I went around the mangled trunk of my hire car and hunkered down where he was hanging upside down in the driver's window. He looked dazed and confused, and very unhappy.

A moment later, Dehan hunkered down next to me, holding the automatic with a handkerchief. She looked at the upside-down face that had started to whimper and said, "Son of a gun, would you look at who it is . . ."

I sighed. "I'd say he has experienced a reversal in his fortunes, wouldn't you, Dehan?"

She nodded at me, blinking. "Both accurate *and* witty, Stone. Droll, even." She turned back to the upside-down face that had now started to sob. There was no sympathy that I could detect, either in her face or in my own feelings. She said, "You know the big difference between U.S. cops and U.K. cops, Sadiq? Shall I tell you what it is? British cops are highly trained in dealing with violence so that it does not escalate. They are trained not to respond to violence with violence, but to defuse it. I think that is an admirable trait, don't you, Stone?"

"I do, Dehan. It's a shame we are not more like that."

"Us?" she went on. "Especially in places like the Bronx, we just shoot shit, don't we, Stone?"

"Mm-hm . . . some guy comes at you with a gun or a knife, or a bad attitude. You shoot him."

"Or a car."

"Or a car."

"So, Sadiq, you come at us, sneaking like a thief in the night, out of the shadows, with a gun, aiming to kill my husband, and his wife, on our honeymoon, what do *you* think we are most likely to do . . . ?"

She put the muzzle of the automatic against his temple and pulled back the hammer with a loud click. He started to cry in earnest.

I said, "Hold on a moment there, Dehan. I'm just thinking, this hard-ass warrior here might actually be useful to us."

"Nah! C'mon! We're going home tomorrow. Just blow his brains out and let the Brits sort it out."

Sadiq made a small whimpering noise. "No, no, he's right, let me help, please, please don't shoot me . . ."

I stood. Dehan sighed. "Come *on,* Stone! Let's just get the hell out of here! It's not our problem!" Suddenly she grabbed the automatic in both hands and aimed. "I'm going to shoot the anti-Semitic son of a bitch!"

I barked, "No! Wait! Just hang on. Jesus, Dehan! Don't you ever get tired of shooting people?"

I managed to pull the door open, drag the whimpering Sadiq out of the car, and dump him on the ground while Dehan gave me a mouthful about saving the city a fortune in legal costs, all the while keeping Sadiq covered.

I checked to see if he had anything broken. He didn't, but he had some handsome bruises.

"So." I smiled at him. "Explain to my Jewish partner here, Sadiq, why she shouldn't do the British taxpayers a big favor and save them the expense of a trial. How exactly are you more useful alive than dead?"

Dehan shook her head. Her face twisted suddenly with savage rage and she snarled, "This son of a bitch is never going to be useful to anybody!" She aimed and pulled the trigger. The two rapid explosions echoed through the trees, and overhead a million terrified wings scattered through the leaves and the branches.

I stared at Dehan in horror. "What the hell have you done . . . ?"

FIFTEEN

We got back to London at eight that evening. While Dehan went up to our room, I explained to the concierge that we had been rear-ended by a large SUV with a French sticker, but the driver had taken off and we hadn't been able to get his license plate. We sorted out the insurance, and I signed the necessary papers and went into the cocktail bar. I ordered a large Bushmills and went to sit in a quiet corner. There, I pulled out my phone and dialed a number. It rang half a dozen times and finally a pleasant, educated voice said, "Hello?"

"May I speak to Nigel Hastings, please?"

There was a pause, then he said, "May I ask who's calling?"

"John Stone."

There was another long pause. "Mr. Stone, I don't believe . . . How can I help you?"

"You were going to say you don't believe you know me?"

His voice hardened. "What is it you want, Mr. Stone?"

"We need to talk."

"I don't think so."

"Then you think wrong. It will not be impossible to trace Sadiq back to you, Hastings. I have his cell, and I am guessing that even if the car is not directly traceable to you, if DI Green keeps following the money, it will not be long before your name pops up."

"I don't know what fantasy you are living, Mr. Stone, but a meeting between you and me is simply not going to happen."

"What fantasy? I'll tell you. It's the fantasy where you haven't hung up on me yet, it's the fantasy where you panic because you hear through the grapevine that I have found Simon Clarence, it's the fantasy where I discover that Dr. Peters is in fact Nigel Hastings, the man who, in 2003, was defense counsel advising Brad Johnson when he was wrongly accused of being the Butcher of Whitechapel, the fantasy where the Butcher was in fact Simon Clarence and you were appointed his legal advisor during his sectioning. Is any of this fantasy making sense to you, Hastings?"

I took a sip of my whiskey. He didn't say anything, but he didn't hang up.

"It's the same fantasy where the hit you ordered on me and my wife went wrong, Sadiq Hassan came off the road, and my Jewish wife was driven beyond endurance and shot the bastard in the head. Now you and I both have a problem. So we need to talk. Am I getting through to you, Hastings?"

He was quiet for a long time. He knew he had a big problem, and he was trying to find a way out of it that did not involve talking to me. There wasn't one, so eventually he said, "Where are you now?"

"At the Ritz."

"Come to Villiers Road, in Willesden..."

"Think again, pal. I was one and a half years with Scotland Yard, remember? I know Willesden, and the only way I go there is with a handful of squad cars. No abandoned warehouses. Let me lay it on the line for you, Hastings. I go back to the States tomorrow. You set the cops hunting for me or my wife and you go down with us. We put the cops on your tail, our involvement in Sadiq's death is your word against ours. So you come here, to the Ritz, and we talk."

"How do I know this isn't a trap?"

"At the Ritz? Seriously? In the cocktail bar at the Ritz?"

"All right, give me half an hour."

"Make it fifteen minutes."

He hung up. I sat thinking, chewing my lip. It was a mess, and it was going to take a cool head and a hell of a lot of skill to sort it out. I called Henry. He sounded tense, but he tried to hide it. "John, what's up, mate?"

"Don't give me any bullshit, Henry. I have no time to waste. I need a straight answer."

I could hear the frown in his voice. "Steady on."

"The sheets."

"*What?*"

"The sheets from Katie's apartment . . ."

"Oh, now, John . . . !"

"Don't do it, Henry. I am more serious than you can imagine. Somebody just tried to kill us. Now give me a straight answer. The traces of DNA on the sheets. You took Sadiq's DNA?"

"Yes."

"The sheets were not a match, were they?"

He hesitated.

I snarled. "Just say yes or no, Henry! Grow a pair, for Christ's sake!"

"No! The profile's not in the system." Then he asked, "Who the hell tried to kill you? What have you been doing, for crying out loud?"

I grunted. "What I should have done fifteen years ago. What we both should have done fifteen years ago. Listen to me . . ."

We talked a little longer, then I hung up. I sipped my drink and ate peanuts, and fifteen minutes later a man, about six foot, average build, dark hair, with a nondescript face, dressed in a charcoal-gray, three-piece, Ede & Ravenscroft pin-striped suit, stepped into the bar. He saw me and approached.

"Mr. Stone?"

"You know damn well I am, Hastings. Sit down. And have a

drink. You're so damn inconspicuous you stand out like a whore at a bishop's convention."

The waiter came over. Hastings glanced at him. "Beefeater and Schweppes." Then he stared at me and I stared back. He said, "What do you want?"

I leaned forward and scowled. "You sent that son of a bitch Sadiq Hassan to kill us. He already had my wife in his sights because she's Jewish. So he was only too happy to do the job when you gave him the contract. But I have news for you, pal, she got him instead."

"Once again, Stone. What do you want?"

"I want a guarantee that you will not come after us. We go back to the States tomorrow, we take what we know with us, and you forget we exist. I want every trace of evidence that you sent Sadiq to kill us erased. I want all and any connection between that bastard and my wife disappeared. Not a trace is to remain. You understand me?"

"Perfectly."

I narrowed my eyes and shook my head. "I'm not hearing it, Hastings. All I'm getting is a British stone wall. What does 'perfectly' mean? You understand me but you're going to try and fuck me anyway?"

"Would you mind moderating your colorful, American language, please, Mr. Stone?"

"I got shot at today, by a man you sent after me. I watched a slug pass within an inch of my wife's head. I then watched her kill the bastard who shot at her. I am not about to moderate my language. What I am about to do is take this eight-ounce whiskey tumbler and rearrange your face with it, if you don't quit trying to be smart. Now, I have told you what I want. So I want to hear an unambiguous answer. Otherwise things start getting ugly. And let me tell you, Hastings, if things get ugly, you go down for fifteen to life."

The waiter appeared and set Hastings' gin and tonic in front of him. Then withdrew.

He stared at his glass awhile, then moved it directly in front of him and turned it around several times, like he was checking it for traps before taking a sip. He raised it to his lips, took a long pull, smacked his lips, and set the glass carefully down again. He was a careful, meticulous man.

"There is very little connecting Sadiq to me or to your wife. We are professional about this kind of thing. However, whatever little there is, I shall make sure it is destroyed. There will be no way at all of connecting him to her. Or to myself, for that matter. In exchange, you leave the country and you never return. You break off all ties with DI Green, and you desist in your investigation into Katie Ellison's death. This is not your jurisdiction, and it is none of your concern." He paused. "If you do not honor this agreement, I will ensure—and believe me, I have the means—that your wife goes to prison for the rest of her life, or that she dies a miserable, painful death, whichever is simplest. Do we have an understanding?"

I nodded. "Yeah, we have an understanding." I took another pull on my whiskey. "Just tell me something." I stared at him and shrugged, squinting my eyes. "Why'd you kill her?"

"Don't be absurd! You're drunk!"

"I'm not drunk! I want to know! How old was she, for God's sake? She was practically a kid! Wasn't there some other way? Couldn't you have made a deal with her?"

"I don't have to listen to this!"

He made to stand. I snarled, "Siddown! You want me to shout my questions across the bar?"

"This was *not* our agreement!"

"Well, I want to know!"

"Keep your voice down, for heaven's sake, man!"

I rasped a whisper at him. "I want to know! Why did you kill her? How dangerous could a kid like that be?"

"That is not your concern, and I have no intention of answering your absurd questions. Now for God's sake, get a grip, man!"

I scowled at him, took another swig, and set my glass down. He watched me do it with distaste. "At least tell me this," I said. "Was she your lover? Was it you she was seeing? Was it you Sadiq called a filthy Jew?"

His face flushed. "I don't need to listen to this."

"It was, wasn't it? Where are your loyalties, Hastings?"

For a moment, there was a flash of real anger in his eyes. "I can assure you they transcend primitive, tribal allegiances to race and religion!"

I nodded. "Oh yeah, I can see that in the allies you choose. Nothing tribal or primitive about Sadiq. Good choice."

He took another swig. His hand was shaking. "Thank you for the drink, Mr. Stone. I hope, for both our sakes, that we never meet again."

He stood, and I watched him walk out of the bar on stiff, angry legs. After that, I finished my whiskey and made my way up to our suite, with a slow burn in my belly. Dehan was in the shower again. I wondered for a moment whether she had washed the gunshot residue from her hands. Then I sat, called reception, and asked for a courier to come and collect a parcel for immediate urgent delivery. I prepared the parcel, and as I was finishing it, Dehan appeared in the bedroom doorway. She was wrapped in a towel and her wet, black hair was hanging around her shoulders. She had a comb in her hand. She watched me a moment.

"Is it done?"

I nodded, then added, "Henry hasn't got our tickets yet."

She started combing her hair. "Did Hastings agree?"

"I think so. We'll have to wait and see."

Our eyes locked for a moment, then she turned and went back into the bedroom to dress. Five minutes later, the courier arrived, and I gave him the parcel with strict instructions. Finally, I went to shower and to dress for dinner.

In the dining room, we sat in a fairly somber mood, which was a shame, because not only is the Ritz dining room spectacular and the food exquisite, but Dehan was wearing a very simple, short black dress with long, silver earrings and a silver chain around her neck that made her look like mortal sin on long, brown legs.

She caught me staring and gave me a rueful look across the table. "Bit of a mess, huh, Stone?"

I shook my head. "You know what? What the hell? It's our last night. Chiddester and Scotland Yard are paying, so let's have a dozen oysters and a bottle of champagne. The way you look right now, it would be a crime not to."

She grinned. "And then the beef Wellington."

I called the waiter and gave him our order. I let him choose the champagne, because I wasn't paying, but told him I wanted a bottle of Vega Sicilia Unico, from the Ribera del Duero region of Spain. The wine list told me it cost seven hundred and seventy pounds sterling, which was just over a thousand dollars. But I figured it was the only chance I was ever likely to get of drinking that legendary wine, so I thanked Chiddie in my heart and went right ahead and ordered it.

Dehan's eyebrows had crawled almost all the way to her hairline. I shrugged. "The Duke of Wellington defeated Joseph Bonaparte at Vitoria, not far from where that wine is made. As we are eating beef Wellington, it seemed appropriate."

She said quietly, "Have you lost your mind?"

"Possibly, but it's your fault for wearing that dress."

She lowered both her eyebrows and then raised just one of them again. She had a mobile face. "Well," she said, "if you're flirting with me, I guess you've forgiven me."

"Forgiven you? I married you because you're a badass, Dehan. You did the right thing."

The oysters arrived, along with a bucket of ice and a bottle of champagne. We toasted, and as we ate and sipped the exquisite wine, our mood began to improve, and our optimism rose. With the beef and the Vega Sicilia, we became positively merry.

We finished the meal, complacent and overfed, with a selection of British cheeses and a thirty-four-year-old Teeling Irish single malt. By that time, we had spent a whole hour not talking about the Katie Ellison case, and I was feeling quite amused by the amount of other people's money we had spent on our honeymoon.

That was when my cell buzzed in my pocket. I offered Dehan an apologetic smile and said, "I'll be right back."

I stepped out into the lobby, put the phone to my ear, and said, "Yeah, Stone."

"Chiddester here. We are on the brink of a major crisis."

"I know."

"You can't leave before it's settled."

"It's not that simple."

"Is it true, what I'm hearing?"

"I don't know what you're hearing, Chiddester."

"That Dehan . . ."

"Is this line secure?"

A hesitation. ". . . Yes."

"Then it's true. But there is more to it than what you might have heard. Who has contacted you?"

"I can't say, but look, I really think you need to get over here."

"Where are you?"

"Holland Park, number five."

"Are you in trouble?"

"Perhaps, I'm not sure. Shall I send a car for you?"

I thought about it for a moment. "If you do, will we get there? Would it be smarter to get a cab, or ask Henry for a car?"

He gave a small, humorless laugh. "Quite the contrary, dear chap. It's no trouble at all. The Home Office provides men like me with cars that are bulletproof and bombproof. Total waste of the taxpayer's money, but I suppose they think it's necessary. In this day and age, with the enemy living in our very midst, perhaps they're right."

"I hear you. Yeah, then perhaps you should send a car."

I returned to the dining room and ordered coffee. It was my turn to smile ruefully. "Party's over, kiddo. Chiddester is sending a car for us. Time to face the music."

SIXTEEN

The waiter informed us that a car had arrived for us from Lord Chiddester. I took Dehan's arm and we stepped out, through the lobby, to the front steps. The car was a Jaguar XE. It was by the door with the engine running and a uniformed chauffeur holding the rear passenger door open for us. Both the car and the driver looked bulletproof.

He drove fast and efficiently, with his eyes on the road and all three mirrors in rapid, successive glances. As we approached Knightsbridge, he said suddenly, "We've picked up a motorbike, sir. I'll try and get rid of him, but if he's still with us by the time we arrive, I'll ask you to stay in the car till I give you the all clear. All right?"

I nodded. "That's fine."

I went to look out the back window, but he said, "Don't look, please, sir. I'd like him to think we're not aware of him."

"Okay..."

There was the usual traffic at Knightsbridge, but it wasn't heavy, and as we moved toward Kensington Road, up ahead the lights turned to amber. Instead of slowing, the driver accelerated fast, with his eyes on the mirror and a nasty smile on his face. The biker, fearing he might lose us if we jumped the lights, hit the gas too. Twenty feet from the lights, our driver braked hard. There was a squeal of tortured rubber and, through the windshield, I saw all the people waiting to cross at the lights stare in horror, wince, and put their hands to their mouths. Behind us, there was another squeal of brakes, a loud thump, and the car shook. Everybody ran to help the biker and our chauffeur slipped across the red lights and continued on toward Holland Park. After a moment, he said, "It's all right, sir. I think we lost him."

Dehan smiled. "You think?"

Holland Park is short and runs in a slight curve from Holland Park Avenue to Abbotsbury Road. There are no more than twenty or thirty houses on it, and one of those is the Greek Embassy. The rest are huge, white, double-fronted Victorian mansions set back from the sidewalk behind five-foot balustrades. We pulled up outside one of those mansions, about a third of the way down, and while the driver got out and opened the door for Dehan, I got out on the other side.

He scanned the street with his right hand behind his back under his jacket and opened the gate for us. "Make it snappy," he said, and we walked fast down the path that cut through the front lawn to the front door, which opened as we arrived.

A man in a black suit wished us a good evening and ushered us into a large entrance hall. It was elaborately Greco-Roman, the way the Victorians liked it, and was painted mainly white and cream, though a deep burgundy carpet covered the hall and climbed a sweeping, white marble staircase to the upper floors. Large, white doors with brass knobs stood on either side of the hall.

We had no coats to give him, so he gestured us to follow him across the hall to the door on the right. He tapped, stepped in, and said, "Detectives Stone and Dehan, sir." Then he stood back for us to enter.

Chiddester was standing by the Victorian fireplace. He looked worried as he watched us come in and the door close behind us.

The room was furnished with comfortable, modern furniture. The chairs and sofa were flanked by tables and attractive lamps.

Sitting in two of the large, comfortable armchairs were Nigel Hastings and Justin Caulfield. I can't say I was surprised; it was what I had expected. Chiddester came forward.

"My dear Dehan." He took her hand. "I am so sorry that all of this has happened during your honeymoon. Please do sit. Can I offer you a drink?"

She told him she was fine, winked at him, and sat. He shook my hand, frowning at me like he wasn't sure what to make of me. I told him I didn't want a drink either. I sat on the arm of Dehan's chair and smiled at Hastings.

"For a man who never wanted to see me again, Hastings, you didn't take long to arrange it."

He managed to put sneering, contempt, hatred, and triumph all into his face at the same time, and screw it up into an ugly smile. "Did you really think that I would allow you to come swaggering into our country, like some sad, old cowboy, shooting and murdering British citizens? Well, perhaps you can get away with that in Mexico and Panama, or whatever other countries you exploit, but not here! Here we have a little thing called accountability. And here, you face the music."

I shrugged almost apologetically. "Well, it wasn't really me." I pointed at Dehan. "It was her. She has a really bad attitude. She's known for it. But to be honest, Hastings, it did kind of look like self-defense." I frowned then at Caulfield. "However, I am a little confused. We have here a shadow cabinet minister, we have the man who a couple of hours ago said he hoped for both our sakes we would never meet again, we have, as far as I can see, no policemen . . ." I spread my hands. "What's going on, Lord Chiddester?"

Caulfield raised his hands and rested them gently on his lap. "Perhaps I had better explain, as it is in fact I who arranged this meeting. Nigel came to me with this rather bizarre story and I have to say I was a little alarmed. Much as I enjoy seeing the government embarrassed, and especially my honorable friend Lord Chiddester, I do not enjoy seeing my country embarrassed. So I called him and suggested that, before this whole thing becomes an international incident, we talk it through and make sure everything is, so to speak, kosher."

Dehan raised an eyebrow at him. "Seriously?"

"Mrs. Stone, why don't we begin with you telling us exactly why you shot and killed Sadiq Hassan?"

Chiddester watched her. He looked distressed. Dehan crossed her long, mortally sinful legs and said, "I have a better idea. Why don't we start at the beginning, and you explain why you have ties to terrorist organizations that employ assassins to kill foreign nationals on British soil?"

Chiddester's face turned to stone and he shifted his stare from Dehan to Caulfield. He looked troubled. "Steady," he said. "In the first place I don't owe you any explanations for how we run the Labour Party. That is absolutely none of your concern. In the second place, I am afraid that the accusations you're making sound like little more than right-wing extremist hysteria."

I chuckled amiably and did my best imitation of Yosemite Sam. "I ain't sayin' that us an' the boys down the Gun Club don't enjoy huntin' us a few gay Marxist mus-leems at the weekend, but that they-er akazay-shun weren't no hysteria, boy."

Caulfield narrowed his eyes at me like he was trying to work out what was going on in my head. Meanwhile, Hastings was staring as though I had just spoke to him in ancient Greek.

"If you think this is some kind of joke . . ."

"*It's* not a joke, Hastings. You are. And I already warned you that you are playing a very dangerous game." I turned to Caulfield. "I'm just wondering how much of this you know, and how much of it is going on behind your back."

He snapped, "How much of what, exactly, Mr. Stone? I have to tell you that you are not endearing yourself to me with this cavalier, gunslinger attitude of yours."

I shook my head. "Oooh, no you don't, Mr. Caulfield. The

only gunslinging that has gone on here has been from your pals at the Whitechapel Marxist Party, under the orders of your fixer, Mr. Hastings here."

"Again, Mr. Stone, I hear a lot of vague, unsubstantiated . . ."

I interrupted him. "Detective Dehan and I went down to Goodnestone Park earlier today, to talk to Simon Clarence . . ." I waited, watching. Caulfield's face was a blank. Hastings had gone white. I went on. "Simon Clarence, with dual American and British nationality, otherwise known as the Butcher of Whitechapel. On the way back, in a remote area of woodland, a dark blue Audi came up behind us at speed, and as it overtook us, the driver fired a gun at us. The bullet missed my wife by inches. I rammed him in self-defense. His car overturned. When I went to get him out, to ensure that he was all right, a struggle ensued and, in self-defense, Detective Dehan shot her intended assassin. He ambushed us and we defended ourselves." Caulfield drew breath but I talked over him. "That man was Sadiq Hassan, of the WMP."

I could see Hastings' hands trembling in his lap. Caulfield looked confused. He turned to face his aide. "Is this true? Did you know about this?"

He shook his head. "It's not the way he is telling it. Sadiq went to try and . . ."

"So you do know this Sadiq Hassan?"

Hastings licked his lips. "The Party has unofficial ties with various left-wing groups . . ."

Caulfield turned in his chair to face Hastings more directly. Chiddester was staring hard at both of them. "So would you kindly explain to us all, Nigel, what this has to do with us, and in particular me. Why was this Hassan character apparently assaulting Mr. and Mrs. Stone?"

Hastings took a deep breath and stared hard at his boss. "Sir, they were going to interview Simon Clarence. The file on Simon Clarence was sealed, and we thought it advisable to discourage Mr. and Mrs. Stone . . ."

"By *shooting* at them, Nigel? These are police officers working in the service of our closest international ally!"

I was getting bored. I said, "Allow me to cut surgically through the bullshit, Mr. Caulfield." He stared at me with serious distaste expressed on his slightly hairy face. I ignored him and went on. "A few nights ago, Lord Chiddester's daughter was murdered. You both know that. The MO used by the killer was almost identical to the MO used fifteen years ago by the Butcher of Whitechapel. I had various reasons for suspecting that Katie had not, in fact, been killed by the same man as those original victims fifteen years ago. In other words, I did not believe she had been killed by the Butcher of Whitechapel. For a start, she did not quite fit the profile for his victims: she was not American and she was a little too short. More compelling was the fact that the killer had misspelled whiskey on the note he had left."

They were both frowning hard. Caulfield said, "You've lost me."

"The Butcher always left a note with a quote from the song 'American Pie.' In it the word whiskey is spelt the Irish and American way, with *e* before the *y*. But in the note we found at Katie's murder, the word whiskey was spelt the English way, with no *e*. That was enough to convince me, but not DI Green, that this was a different killer. And that got me wondering where the original killer had been for the last fifteen years, and what had happened to the investigation after I had returned to the U.S.A.

"I won't go into the details, but I soon discovered that the Butcher of Whitechapel had pretty much surrendered himself to the authorities, and was being held, at Her Majesty's leisure, at Goodnestone Park." I paused and shook my head. "Very, very few people knew that, because the file had been sealed to protect Simon Clarence's identity. One of the only people who *did* know that was the man employed as his counsel, to protect his interests during the hearings in chambers, when he was sectioned. That happened to be the same man who acted as Brad Johnson's counsel when he was Scotland Yard's prime suspect in the case.

Perhaps that was why he was chosen, because he had that specialized knowledge. In any case, that man was . . ." I pointed at him. "Nigel Hastings."

Caulfield turned to him. "Nigel . . . ?"

Nigel was sweating like a vicar in a sauna full of nuns. "It is true, in substance, but it proves—and *means*—nothing!"

I barged right on. "We'll come to what it proves and what it means in a bit. But the fact is that as we were leaving that meeting, an associate of Hastings' tried to kill us."

Caulfield raised his hands again. "Just slow down a bit, Stone, will you! You keep going on about this connection between Nigel and this Hassan character. But in fact we have nothing but your word for that!"

Dehan said, "Really? Let me ask you a question, Hastings. Suppose I got on Google and started researching your family history. Suppose I got a pro to do it? Suppose, even better, a couple of days ago, when Stone saw you at Caulfield's phony office on Little College Street, suppose I had got a private investigator to do some research into your family? What would he have found?"

"I have no idea what you're driving at, and I find this line of questioning deeply offensive!"

"Would he have found, perhaps, that you have Jewish ancestry that you try to keep secret?"

A quick spasm of anger flashed across Caulfield's face. "What has this to do with anything? Hastings is an ancient English name!"

"As far as I am aware, Caulfield, there have been Jews in England for almost a thousand years, almost as long as there have been Normans. How can you make that distinction?"

His jaw worked but no sound came out. Finally, he said, "What has this to do with anything?"

I shrugged. "Just that when we talked to Sadiq the first time, he said that Katie was involved with a Jewish guy. He called him a lot of other things too, but in essence it boiled down to the same thing, Sadiq was mad at her for having what he called a Jewish boyfriend. But as much as we asked, nobody, except Sadiq, knew who he was. So I kept wondering who this guy could be. And, like a lot of men who try to stay anonymous, Hastings just kept popping up all over the place."

Hastings was shaking his head like a wet dog. "No, no, no! You have absolutely no evidence whatsoever that I was in any kind of relationship with Lord Chiddester's daughter. None! You can't even show that I *knew* her! Let alone had a relationship with her! This is all the wildest, most unsubstantiated surmise! It is *outrageous*!"

Sometimes in life, things happen right on cue. Most times they don't, and this was one of those times when they didn't. So I had to take a long shot.

"When Katie was killed, DI Green, Dehan, and I all agreed that it was important to test Katie's sheets for DNA residue." I shook my head and smiled at Dehan. "Remember when we told Sadiq we planned to do that?"

She smiled at Hastings. "We thought he was going to have a seizure. We took that to mean we were going to find *his* DNA. But he was going on and on about this Jewish guy who had been seeing Katie . . ." She shook her head. "It was very confusing. Especially as he was *the only* person who seemed to know who he was."

I spread my hands. "We rushed the tests through private clinics, thanks to Lord Chiddester's resources, and when the results came in they showed, to our surprise, that Sadiq had not been sleeping with Katie.

"But, did you know? Israel has been using certain genetic profiles to determine who has a right to claim Israeli citizenship for some years. And let me tell you, the guy who had been sleeping with Katie has that right. He is not, perhaps, of the Jewish faith, but he is nonetheless genetically of Jewish descent."

I was staring right at Hastings as I was speaking. His face

flushed with anger. "What makes you so determined that I am Jewish! *I am not Jewish!* What is *wrong* with you?"

"Your DNA profile says otherwise."

He shook his head. "How could you possibly know that? I have never *had* my DNA profiled."

"Oh, you have, this afternoon."

"*What?*"

"You kindly left it on your gin and tonic glass. I rushed it to the lab. The latest technology is very fast, when you have access to it. Less than four hours. And your profile matches that left at Katie's apartment. You *are* the Jewish guy she was sleeping with, that Sadiq hated so much."

He covered his face with his hands. "The *fucking* gin and tonic . . . !"

Chiddester spoke suddenly, staring at Hastings with crazy eyes.

"So you killed my little girl . . ."

SEVENTEEN

Caulfield got to his feet suddenly and strode away across the large room with his hands behind his back. The drapes were closed, so instead of looking out at the dark street, he stopped dead and looked down at his feet. Eventually he turned and stared hard at the back of Hastings' head.

"The damage you have done the party is *incalculable*, Nigel. I will disown you completely. Your actions are beneath contempt. How you could put the party at risk in this way, it is beyond words."

Dehan was nodding. "Yeah, because *that's* what's important. Screw the fact that he murdered a young woman and destroyed her family. Hey, that's collateral damage in the all-important political war, right, Caulfield? What counts here is that this schmuck put the party at risk. *That* is the real crime."

Caulfield stared at her for a moment, then at Chiddester, who seemed to have gone into a trance. Slowly, grotesquely, the politician seemed to claw his way out of Caulfield's face. "You are absolutely right, Mrs. Stone. I have expressed myself in a very regrettable way. Politics gets to the most human of us eventually. Lord Chiddester, you have my deepest sympathy, and naturally the Labour Party will do everything in its power to help . . ."

Chiddester didn't look at him. He growled at an empty space a few feet in front of his face. "I don't need your help. My daughter is dead. Nothing can ever change that." He turned to look at Hastings. "And that man killed her, in the service of the toxic, twisted culture at the heart of your party." He pointed a trembling finger at Caulfield. "You are as responsible as he is. You may as well have pulled the trigger yourself. She was killed trying to expose your sick culture of totalitarian Marxism and your grotesque allegiance to Islamic extremism. You are a traitor to your country, a traitor to your people, a traitor to democracy, and complicit in the murder of a good, beautiful girl. I hope you rot in hell, Caulfield!"

Caulfield had gone white. "Steady on there, Chiddester..."

Chiddester's face flushed suddenly crimson. "If you think you are going to use this sniveling piece of *shit* as a scapegoat, and walk away from your crimes scot-free, you are sadly deluded! I am going to *destroy* you, and your party! There will not be another Labour government as long as I live!" He raised his arm and his hand was trembling with rage. "I will make it my business to expose all of your treachery, your treason, your crimes against the people. *How stupid do you think the British public is?*" Suddenly he was shouting, almost screaming. "*What fucking inferences do you think they will draw, when they read it in the papers, when they see it on the national news, that Katie Ellison was murdered by a member of your filthy party of treasonous, anti-Semitic lackeys to the Islamic State, because she was going to uncover your ties to Marxist groups and Islamic fundamentalists? What inference do you think they will draw, Caulfield?*"

His voice stopped abruptly and a ringing silence was left in its place. He moved across the room and lowered himself onto the sofa.

Caulfield stared at him in what looked like genuine shock. After a moment, he stammered. "But, he was working alone, Chiddester. You must see that. The Labour Party would never sanction an operation like that . . . You can't drag the whole party into this. We had no knowledge."

"You created the conditions for it to happen. You seeded the rot, you fostered the madness, you created the culture of apologism for Islamic atrocities. You and your spineless, power-grubbing supranationalists. Get out of my house, you make me sick."

Hastings suddenly spoke up. "Hang on a second. What about these two? They murdered Sadiq. The deal was they kept their mouths shut and we didn't go after the Je . . . after Mrs. Stone for killing Sadiq!"

I smiled at Caulfield. "Boy, you are going to be a big loss to the march of civilization."

He didn't smile back. "He has a point."

"What do you suggest, Caulfield?"

He didn't answer me; he spoke to Chiddester.

"Look, for God's sake, Chiddester, you're talking about tearing apart the whole political fabric of the country. Let this couple go home. After all, it seems that Mrs. Stone was in fact acting in self-defense. There is no need to prosecute them, let them have their lives. Sadiq has paid for his crime, Nigel must pay for his, and we'll see to that. But for God's sake, let's do some damage limitation and leave it at that . . ."

Dehan looked at me. "He wants to let us have our lives, Stone. Is that what they call magnanimity?"

Chiddester spoke before I could answer. "Damage limitation? What I am talking about, you disgusting little man, is uprooting the festering roots of the poisoned ivy you have seeded in our society. I am talking about tearing them up and showing them to the people, in all their horrific ugliness, so that the likes of you will never come to power again!"

He looked at me and I nodded. He stood and walked to the fireplace, where he pressed a bell in the wall. A moment later the door opened and the man who had let us in said, "Yes, M'Lord?"

"Bring him in."

The door closed, and Caulfield looked at me and Dehan, then at Chiddester. "What is this? What are you doing, Chiddester?"

"I am shining a light," snarled Chiddester, "on the swarming rats and cockroaches that claim to represent the working people of this country!"

A moment later, the door opened and the servant, accompanied by a young man in his early twenties, stepped into the room. Between them, they held Sadiq Hassan.

Hastings' face crumbled and he began to sob into his hands like a child. Caulfield gaped. "You treacherous . . ."

"You dare to call me treacherous, you murdering bastard?"

I smiled. "We scared the living daylights out of him and left his ears ringing. Well, Dehan did, but we didn't shoot him, despite being gun-totin' cowboys. Maybe it's time you revised some of your stereotypes, huh, Hastings? See, we figured, if you thought you had something over us, if you thought there could be some give-and-take, you might just give, and you did. You gave your DNA, and you gave a confession." I held Caulfield's eye for a long moment, then I said, "So here's the thing I'm curious about, Caulfield. Here we are, two cops without jurisdiction, a backbench Member of Parliament, a member of a Marxist group who has close ties to Islamic extremists, a prime suspect in Katie Ellison's murder, and you, a shadow cabinet minister. What do you propose we should do next?"

He returned to his chair and sat staring at the floor, chewing his lip. Hastings looked at me and said, "I swear I did not kill her. I was very fond of her."

Dehan gave him a look that could have castrated a bull and said, "Shut up, Adolph."

Caulfield spoke to the carpet, with both hands stuck out like he was holding an invisible box.

"What will it take, Chiddester? Men like us, though we may be bitterly opposed to each other's ideals, we must see the bigger picture. What happened to your daughter is an outrageous crime, and the man, or men, responsible must and will be brought to justice. But can't you see the crises that will enfold our society if the Labour Party is brought down?" He suddenly looked at me and at Dehan, appealing to us. "Imagine if in the States the entire Democratic Party were brought down. It would be a devastating blow not just to the left, but to the country as a whole!"

I grunted. "So what are you proposing?"

He closed his eyes. "I admit, there has been an issue in the party with anti-Semitism, and I will hold up my hand and say clearly, we should all have been more vigilant, more aware of the problem. I will give you my personal undertaking, my word, that we will address this problem . . ."

I interrupted him. "What about the ties to Islamic fundamentalism?"

His mouth worked but no words came out. Sadiq was staring at him fixedly. "I am not aware that any such ties . . ."

I pointed at Sadiq and half shouted. "You're looking at one right now, Caulfield! This man right here, who tried to murder us, he *is* a tie between you and Islamic fundamentalism. He was carrying out hits for the Labour Party, for crying out loud!"

"No . . ." He was shaking his head. "No, no, no! He and Hastings were operating without the sanction of the party!"

I shouted, "*Total deniability, huh? Is that what you had? And what did you promise in exchange?*"

"No! You can't do this! We are the Parliamentary Labour Party, for God's sake! We are the establishment!"

A deathly silence lay on the room. I pulled my phone from my pocket and dialed. After a moment, I said, "Henry? We have Hastings here. We'll hold him till you arrive." Then I turned to Sadiq. "Get the hell out of here. Try and find the passages in your book that talk about universal love for all people, despite their religion."

He spat at my feet. "There aren't any, filthy Jew-loving pig!"

He turned and walked out of the room, slamming the doors as he went. Finally, I looked at Caulfield. "Get out, Caulfield. You make me nauseous. It's depressing that people can be like you.

Even if you had no hand in this murder, what Lord Chiddester says is true, you created the conditions for this corruption to flourish. You are beneath contempt. Get out."

He stood, and his legs were trembling. He walked out of the room with a strange, stiff gait and again we heard the door slam.

Hastings looked at me resentfully. "Why do they get to go home, and I get arrested? You know full well they are as guilty as I am."

It was Dehan who answered. "That's what happens to fall guys, schmuck."

"Besides," I said, "you really figure Sadiq for the heroic type? We delivered him to Lord Chiddester on the way back from Kent. Before we got there, he was saying he wanted to turn Queen's evidence. He's on his way now with a couple of cops to collect all the evidence Katie had put together. He told us he'd collected it from her apartment after . . ."

Hastings' eyes were swiveling this way and that like they had a life of their own. He blurted out, "That's not right, that's *wrong*. Why would *he* have her stuff?"

"Well if he hasn't, who has?"

The question was obvious and so was the answer, and if he hadn't been in such a panic, he would have seen he was being led. But he was too scared to see the nose in front of his own face.

"Obviously I have it! I killed her, to shut her up! And I have her stuff! That's obvious, isn't it!"

I frowned. "Can you prove that?"

"Of course I can prove it! I have everything—her laptop, her memory sticks, her notebooks. Everything! It's all at . . . !" He faltered, realizing too late he had been trapped.

I laughed. "The whole thing, Hastings—calling you to the Ritz, Chiddester's call to me when you showed up, as you had to —the whole thing was planned. And you walked right in."

Chiddester looked gray and exhausted. He said suddenly, "All right, Green. You may as well come in now. I think we have everything we need."

Hastings' eyes bulged. He scrambled to his feet and ran for the door. Chiddester was quick for a man his size, and strong. He stood, laid the flat of his left hand on Hastings' chest, and stopped him dead in his track. Then he delivered a right hook to his jaw that sent him reeling back across the room and laid him flat on his back, groaning like Sunday morning after Saturday night.

"There'll be no Queen's evidence in this case. You're all going to the *fucking wall*!"

The doorbell rang and the guys who'd brought Sadiq in went to open it. There was a murmuring of voices and a rustling of feet, and after a moment the door opened again and Henry came in with two constables.

"Evening, all. Where is he?"

Chiddester pointed and said, "He tried to get away. Had to stop him." The constables crossed the room and dragged Nigel Hastings to his feet. He was still having trouble focusing his eyes, and he had an ugly, swollen bruise covering the lower left side of his face. The constables cuffed him, and Henry intoned, "Nigel Hastings, I am arresting you on suspicion of the murder of Katie Ellison, and conspiring in the attempted murder of Detectives John Stone and Carmen Dehan. You do not have to say anything, but it may harm your defense if you do not mention when questioned something which you later rely on in court. Anything you do say may be given in evidence against you." He nodded at the constables. "All right, take him away."

As they walked him past me, Henry said, "Oh, by the way, Stone, the DNA results came in last minute. It was Hastings' DNA, like you thought."

He stopped and stared at me with crazy eyes. "You tricked me! You're all the same! Lying, cheating . . ."

The rest of it was lost as he was bundled out into the hall. Chiddester frowned down at Dehan, who was still sitting in her chair in her sinful black dress. "I'm sorry you had to witness that, my dear."

I smiled down at her, wondering if she'd give him a taste of her attitude. But there was only humor in her eyes. She stood and grinned at him and said, "Don't apologize, Chiddie. I just wish I'd filmed it so I could watch it again."

She winked and his cheeks flushed. Henry made a "crazy Yanks" face and said, "Right, we'd better be making a move. Lord Chiddester, I'll leave a car outside and an armed officer inside. Any problem at all . . ."

"And I'll shoot the bastard, Green, don't worry about that."

I smiled, and before Henry could reprimand him, I asked, "Where is your wife, Chiddester?"

"Upstairs in bed. We'll be fine, now go and do whatever you have to do."

We stepped out into the balmy night and crossed the garden toward Henry's car. The street was oddly peaceful, with the ancient, wrought iron streetlamps casting a gentle, green light through the leaves of the giant chestnuts. His car bleeped and flashed and we pulled open the doors. Then he leaned on the roof a moment and looked at me. "Tough old goat, isn't he? Lost his daughter, obviously shattered by it, and yet there he is, in the thick of it, not flinching, and even decks the fellow who did it."

I nodded. "A few more like him, huh, Henry?"

He shrugged. "Maybe. Maybe you're right."

EIGHTEEN

The radio crackled in the darkness of the car:

"Subject moving north along Ladbroke Grove. Over."

We pulled away and headed toward Holland Park Avenue. Henry took the radio and spoke. "Bravo team, what is the status of your subject? Over."

"Bound west along the Acton Vale, sir, seems to be headed home to Ealing Common. Over."

We reached the intersection with Holland Park Avenue and stopped. It was late and there was no traffic. The road was quiet and still.

I said, "Caulfield has gone home. Sadiq is on his way to Villiers Road, in Willesden."

He looked at me sharply. "How do you know that?"

I sighed. I could explain, but it wouldn't convince him. I said, "Believe me. Leave the tail on Caulfield, there is an outside chance he's not involved. We know for a fact Sadiq is. Even if I'm wrong, which, you know, I'm not, we should stay with him."

He sighed and turned north toward Notting Hill Gate. "Couldn't you be wrong just sometimes?" he said, with not much humor. He turned left then, and we started accelerating down Ladbroke Grove, toward the Harrow Road. It is long and straight, and at that time of night, there were few people about. The luminous shop fronts and kebab parlors gave the street a depressing air of hopelessness. We passed under the metro bridge and the radio crackled again.

"Subject headed for Kensal Rise Station. There is no traffic, sir, we are falling back in case he spots us. Over."

"Roger that, Sergeant."

I turned to him. "Kensal Rise is on the way to Willesden, isn't it?"

He nodded and gave a glance in the mirror. I heard Dehan laugh.

"Left onto Staverton . . . He's doing another left onto Willesden Lane, sir. Over."

Henry sighed. "Be advised, he is probably headed for Villiers Road. Alpha One, stay behind him. Alpha Two, take Belton Road and intercept at the junction with Villiers. Over."

"Roger that, sir."

It crackled again almost immediately. "Bravo team, sir. Subject has stopped at the Guilded Lilly on Ealing Broadway. All night bar, sir. Over."

"Stay with him, Bravo team, and stay in your vehicles! Over."

He hit the gas and we crossed the Grand Union Canal doing seventy. We crossed the Harrow Road against the lights and climbed at speed through Kilburn, past the station, and onto Chamberlayne Road. Ten minutes later, he slowed as we eased onto Willesden Lane and he pulled up at the corner.

"Stay here, please."

He got out and crossed the sidewalk, moving along Villiers Road. Three cars in, he hunkered down and the driver's window slid down. Dehan leaned over my right shoulder so we could both look down the street. It was straight for about three hundred yards, then turned left at somewhat less than a right angle. Where it made the bend, on the right, there was a large iron gate that I guessed gave onto a courtyard.

Henry stood and peered down the road. I knew what he was

looking for because I had already found it while he was talking. He came back, climbed in, and slammed the door.

"He drove into a courtyard, on the bend. It seems there are a couple of warehouses there. The idea of being a consultant, John, is that you share and cooperate, you know."

"You sacked me, remember? You sent me home."

"Whatever."

He fired up the engine and we cruised gently down the road to an empty parking space twenty yards from the gate on the opposite side. There he stopped and killed the engine.

"Now we wait, and pray to God that you're right."

We were quiet for a bit, then Dehan asked suddenly, "Since when have British Socialists been anti-Semitic? I would never have thought of the British as anti-Semitic, least of all the Socialists!"

He shrugged. "I'm not sure they are, but there has been a growing faction in the Labour Party, over the last few decades. It all started at more or less the same time: we joined the EU, EEC as it was back then, there was the big petrol crisis—you're too young to remember that, but basically OPEC cut off the supply of oil to the U.K., and next thing there were thousands of oil billionaires buying up Britain, everything from Harrods to half the property in Kensington." He looked in the mirror at her. "I'm not a political animal. I think anyone who wants to be a politician should be automatically disqualified. But barroom politicians, and there are plenty in this country, suspect that they bought up a bit more than just Harrods and Kensington real estate. I couldn't say, but roughly around that time, there began to be an anti-Israeli feeling in the country, not so much in the pubs as on the BBC and among certain politicians. Whether they were right or wrong, I couldn't say, but the consensus at the King's Arms, my local, is that more than one politician, on *both* sides of the House, mind, gets his or her orders, and his paycheck, from Riyadh."

I raised an eyebrow at him. "That is dangerous talk for a cop, Henry."

He shrugged. "Like I said, I don't know anything about politics. I'm just telling you what the lads down the pub think."

Half to myself, I asked, "How many uprisings and revolutions started in pubs, I wonder."

His reply was immediate. "All of them."

Then he raised his hand and we went silent. Headlamps were approaching down the road. They slowed as they approached the corner, then turned in at the iron gates. I could now make out it was a dark Mercedes A-Class Saloon. Nobody got out, but after a moment, the gates began to open, and the car slipped in, parked, and killed the lights. Then a figure climbed out and walked to a darkened door, where it knocked and waited.

I suddenly went cold and my skin crawled. Henry was frowning. He grabbed the radio. "Bravo team, what is the status of your subject? Over."

"He's still in the club, sir. We have clear eyes on his car and the door, and he hasn't come out . . ."

"What was he driving?"

"Audi A8, sir. Over."

"Who the fuck's that?"

"Whoever it is, is going to kill Sadiq in the next ten minutes if we don't do something."

He stared at me a moment. "A hit man? Called from the club?"

I frowned. "What's he got, a damned army?"

He grabbed the radio. "Alpha One, move in up to the gates. No lights. Alpha Two, hold your position. Both of you, be prepared to intercept fugitives."

"Roger!"

"Let's go."

We scrambled out of the car. I noticed Dehan had dumped her shoes and was barefoot. I grinned. "When I told you dress for the evening, this isn't what I meant."

"I know that now."

Henry was already loping across the road. Dehan was close

behind him. He turned to me. "Now how do we get through the damned gate?"

I was halfway across the road, walking. "I know a technique. It's pretty smart, but I need your permission to try it."

"Be my guest, only hurry, will you?"

"Give me your car keys."

He tossed them to me and I ran a couple of steps back to the car. I fired up the engine, put it in reverse, and gave the steering wheel full lock. The car whined backward into the middle of the road. I tried not to laugh when I saw Henry's face. I lined up the trunk with the gate and floored the pedal. The crash and scream of twisted steel was horrific. It made a real mess of the trunk, but it opened the gate, and I like to think it may have saved Sadiq's life.

As I climbed out of the cab and threw him his keys, Henry was shouting at me, "*Are you out of your fucking mind?*"

"Sue me. No time for this now. Let's go!"

We ran for the door. I noticed absently it was the Al-Fakiha Import Company, which struck me as eminently appropriate. I put my elbow through the glass pane, reached in, and turned the handle. Next thing, we were in a small office. It was dark, but by the filtered light of the streetlamps I could make out a shabby desk, a couple of chairs, and an old telephone. On the left there was a black, impenetrable oblong: a doorway into the bowels of the building.

Henry spoke into his radio. "Alpha Two, we need backup. Gate is open, as is door, both courtesy of the U.S. Demolition Squad."

"Roger!"

I whispered, "Did anybody bring a flashlight or a gun?"

"I imagine our friends in there brought both."

Dehan said, "Why don't we just turn on the light?"

She flipped the switch and flooded the room with light. We could now see through the open doorway, a short distance down a concrete corridor. There I could make out a large set of double doors. They had the look of warehouse doors. I moved toward them. As I stepped into the passage, I saw there were stairs on the left leading up to the next floor. I shook my head at Henry. "You need to call in a firearms unit, Henry. If either of them has a gun, we are sitting ducks."

I heard the crunch of feet behind us. Three uniforms were making their way in, led by a giant sergeant. They at least were wearing body armor.

"I'll call it in," he said. "But it could take at least an hour to get a firearms team here, if they send one. We actually have no real reason other than your bloody colon to believe they're armed." He turned to the uniforms. "Sergeant Lewis, go upstairs and see if there's anyone there. Employ extreme caution, one or both of them may be armed."

"Yes, gov."

They started making their way up the stairs. I pushed open the doors to the warehouse. It was a large, cavernous, dark space. The air was chill.

I called out, "*Sadiq! The place is surrounded! We have a firearms team on its way! You are not going anywhere. Give it up and hand over the material.*"

There was only silence. I stepped in and peered to my right. The vast nave filtered away into shadows, with stacks of boxes piled against the walls. Dehan tapped my arm and pointed over to the left, where there was a small clapboard and glass office in the corner. I nodded, nudged Henry, and pointed, indicating he should go left and I would go right. Dehan scowled at me and shrugged with a "what about me?" look. I gestured at her dress with both hands. She showed me a finger; it wasn't the one her ring was on.

Henry shouted again, "*Give it up, Sadiq! You're surrounded! Come out with your hands in the air!*"

While he was shouting, I sprinted across the open space to a stack of boxes and took cover behind them. I could make out

Arabic writing as well as English. It said they were full of dates. I was maybe fifteen feet from the office door.

I looked over at Henry and gave him the thumbs-up, then I started shouting, "*Don't make this worse than it is, Sadiq! Cooperate and maybe you can strike a deal! Turn Queen's evidence!*"

I saw Henry dart toward the side of the office and slide below the window. I slipped around the back of the boxes and saw another stack, about six feet from the office door. These were wooden crates, about six feet by four, and had pictures of melons on them. I moved up, caught Henry's eye, and prepared to storm the door.

That was when the glass in the window shattered and Sadiq stood and opened up on me with an assault rifle. I swore violently and rolled behind the crates. A voice was screaming. It was Sadiq, shouting in Arabic, interspersed with English, about how we would never take him alive. Then he shouted, "*Allahu Akbar!*" and opened up with the assault rifle again.

I glanced over at Dehan to make sure she was okay. She was pointing frantically at the crates of melons I was pressed up against. I shrugged and spread my hands. She gritted her teeth, glared, and pointed again. Meanwhile I could hear Sadiq shouting something that sounded very dangerous to me.

"*Where is your firearms unit? Where is your backup? I am going to kill you all! Allahu Akbar!*"

And he opened up again, spraying the area with a hot hail of lead. As I curled up behind the crates, wondering how long it would take the slugs to tear through the melons and find me, I also began to wonder where the hell he'd got an assault rifle from, between Chiddester's house and here. And then, as the noise of lead hitting steel began to dawn on me, I realized what Dehan had been pointing at.

Next thing, I was on my feet, dragging the topmost box to the floor. From the corner of my eye, I saw Dehan break cover and run. A hail of bullets trailed her, kicking up cement dust from the concrete. The box hit the floor and shattered. I heard Sadiq bellowing, coming closer. I looked down and saw the damned box was full of melons.

Sadiq came skidding around the corner, training what looked like an AK-47 on me. I didn't think. He fired as I dropped, and I felt the hot whiz and pop of the slugs skimming past me and into the wood. I grabbed the nearest melon like a football and hurled it straight into his face. It made a sickening thud, and he went over on his back. I leapt at him, pinned down his gun hand with my left knee, and drove my fist into his face, not once and not twice, but three times.

But he was clawing at me with his left, and as he did that, his right arm slipped out from under my knee. Next thing, he was using the AK-47 as a club, writhing underneath me, trying to beat my brains out with the butt. I wrestled it from him, tearing and biting at his fingers. Finally, I wrenched it out of his hands and threw it blindly behind me. I heard it clatter on the cement and started pounding his face again, left, right, and left. He stopped moving. I drew breath and heard Henry shouting at me, "*John! Stop!*"

I looked up at him with my fist poised for a fourth and final blow, but I realized then that he wasn't looking at me. He was looking behind me, and he looked worried. That was when I heard the unmistakable, slightly sneering voice saying, "Don't stop on my account, kill the little shit if you want to."

I lowered my fist, then got to my feet and turned. He was leaning against the shattered wooden crates, holding an automatic in his hand. "I hope you don't mind, DI Green, I left your men sitting outside the club, watching my car, and I borrowed the owner's Merc. He's an old chum of mine."

"Caulfield. I knew it had to be you."

"Well, that makes you very clever, Stone, but sadly, I'm the one holding the gun."

NINETEEN

He aimed the automatic at my head. "On your knees."

I stuck out my lower lip, like I was doubtful, then shook my head. "No, if I'm going to die, Caulfield, I'll do it on my feet, not on my knees."

"How very admirable. It would be so much more admirable if you didn't keep two-thirds of the planet on *their* knees." He waved his gun at Henry. "Cuff him."

"Countries like Saudi Arabia, Caulfield? Countries like the Emirates?"

"I am not going to discuss politics with a gun-toting U.S. hit man."

Henry pulled my arms behind my back, and as he closed the cuffs he said, "Um, actually, Caulfield. You're the one toting the gun, and the only hit men in this affair were employed by you . . ."

"Shut up, Green. Stone, sit down or I'll shoot you in the knee. Green, get on your toy radio and tell your men to back away. Tell them I want a negotiating team dispatched. Then take your shoes and socks off."

Henry got on his radio. "Alpha teams One and Two, be advised we have a hostage situation. Alpha One, fall back to the perimeter. Alpha Two, adopt standard fallback procedure, Sergeant Lewis' discretion. Hostage taker has requested a negotiation team."

I moved over to one of the boxes of dates and sat on it. Now I could see what it was Dehan had been pointing at. The bottommost crate had been torn to kindling by Sadiq's gunfire, and you could see the alternating butts and muzzles of assault rifles poking out.

"What is it, Caulfield, one in every ten cases is guns? Who are they for? Don't tell me you're planning a coup."

"Nothing so dramatic, Stone. There will not be 'rivers of blood' in the streets in dear old Blighty. Not many, anyway. Just enough to keep a certain level of terror alive, to keep the people pliant."

"So you arrange the sales to them, then they ship the guns back to people like Sadiq, so he can shoot the workers you represent in the streets of your city. Is that what they call government for the people?"

"I am well past being upset by your cynicism, Stone. You, Green, sit on the floor next to your buddy. Now here's how it's going to go. I need a jet fueled and ready to go within the next ninety minutes, at London Elstree airport. We will be flying to Saudi. I will give the pilot his instructions once we are aboard. You both will be handed over to the authorities when we arrive. Any delays, or attempts at trickery, and I will take something random off you. It might be a toe, a finger, an ear, an eye, a foot. I will steadily dismember you until you are both dead. That is the deal. When the negotiator arrives, you will persuade him that I am serious, and if he tries to play me, I will take a piece of you. Do you understand, Green?"

Green sighed and nodded. "I do."

I spoke suddenly and loudly. "So, let me see if I have understood this. You are basically employed by who? Al-Qaeda?"

"I am not just employed by them, Stone, I happen to have a certain ideological allegiance with them. I like their certainty, their clarity. I like the fact that they are not afraid to stand up against the Jewish conspiracy. The one area where Marx went wrong was in his atheism. What makes a society strong, what unites a society, is a powerful ideology. And let's face it, few ideologies, if any, are quite as powerful as Islam."

I gave a small laugh. "Save it for the sheep, Pastor. Bottom line is Al-Qaeda pays your salary. So why the Marxism? You've been in the Labour Party all your life, why the ties with Marxists?"

He laughed out loud. "Have you any idea how many Labour MPs and Labour supporters are Marxists? My dream, the dream of many—and you can raise that cynical eyebrow all you like, it does not change the fact—my dream is for a Marxist Britain guided by the spiritual light of Islam." He laughed again, shaking his head. "And believe me, it is very far from being an impossible dream. And I am not alone in dreaming it. Islam is for all humanity, salvation is for all those who embrace it, and the same is true of Marxism."

"That's very nice, Caulfield. I get a nice, warm feeling when I hear you talk that way. Fortunately, not all Muslims are crazy like you. So, how did it go? Katie started investigating the ties between Islam and Marxism in this country, and she hooked up with Sadiq, seduced him, and persuaded him to introduce her to the man who was running him, Hastings. She and Hastings got it on, and I am guessing Sadiq got jealous and told her he was Jewish, not realizing she wouldn't give a damn. How am I doing?"

"You're doing very well. Men like Sadiq have a kind of radar. Some SS officers developed the same kind of instinct during the Third Reich. I have no racial objection to Jews. I am not racist in any way. I am quite objective about the whole thing. It is their dangerous, unstable thinking that troubles me, and their control of the banks."

"That's objective?"

"Very, I assure you."

"So Katie made the mistake of getting sweet on Hastings.

There is no accounting for taste. And Hastings alerted you to the fact that she was on your trail and was gathering evidence . . ."

"Oh, it was much worse than that. She was very clever indeed. With her father's help and connections, and her own talent for investigation, she had put together irrefutable paper trails showing . . ." He stopped and shook his head.

"Showing what? C'mon, Caulfield! You really think I believe you are going to let us live? We are as dead as though you'd already pulled the trigger. Showing what? That you and your buddies . . ."

"Enough, Stone. What she managed to prove will never be known, because her research, and this whole warehouse, will go up in smoke before morning."

"Al-Fakiha."

He frowned at me. "I beg your pardon?"

"What does it mean? You have it plastered all over these boxes."

He laughed. "Oh, it means the fruit. The fruit of our labors, the fruit of our struggle, the fruit of our submission to God. That is what Islam means, you know? Submission. Submission brings God's grace. The fruit."

"That's beautiful. I guess men like me who refuse to get on our knees, we don't stand a chance, huh?"

He shook his head.

I shrugged. "So, when Hastings revealed the extent of Katie's research, you decided she had to die, and you ordered Hastings to do it . . ."

"He volunteered. He really is a very peculiar young man. He was a barrister for many years, you know? Very clever. But a little unbalanced. As you know, he was involved with the Butcher case all those years ago, and it affected him deeply, especially when he met Simon Clarence."

I nodded. "That makes sense. The Home Office were keeping an eye on Johnson, so as assistant to the shadow home secretary, he got to hear that Johnson was back, and that gave him the idea.

He arranged to go and visit Simon and get the details of the killings. That way he could stage it as the return of the Butcher, knowing that the file was sealed and nobody could ever open it up as long as Clarence lived. If he'd just got the spelling of whiskey right, he might have got away with it."

He shrugged. "Too bad for him, really." He frowned at Henry and checked his watch. "What's happening with that negotiating team, Green?"

"First they'll have to assemble it, then there'll be a briefing. You can be sure they're scrambling, sir. Scotland Yard will be shitting bricks. We've asked for the help of a New York copper and now he's a hostage, and being flown to fucking Saudi!"

Caulfield gazed at me. "If he's lucky."

"So what now, Caulfield? Your life's dream is ashes. What will you do? Go and live in a cave in Afghanistan? Your SAS boys will hunt you down, you know? There is nowhere for you to hide."

He smiled, and it was frightening how complacent he was. "Don't worry about me, Stone. I'll survive, and, like Arny, I'll be back. Britain has a destiny. It will be Marxist, and more than that, it will be Muslim, and it will submit to Sharia law."

I shrugged. "You may be right, Caulfield, but you know what? Your pal Marx once said that history repeats itself, and when I look at the history of Britain, I see a tough, smart people who have a lot of common sense, who are slow to anger, but fearsome when roused. And I see a people who over and over again have taken their tyrants and their despots and kicked their asses. I don't see their destiny as one of submission. I think these crazy island people are going to take your vision of destiny and they are going to shove it right up your ass. What do you think, Dehan?"

I had seen her step out from behind the crate with her small, black dress and her sinfully long legs, her hair tied in a knot behind her neck and the AK-47 in her hands. Let me tell you, it was one of the most indecent sights I have ever seen, and I doubt I will ever be lucky enough to see anything like it again, except in my recurring dreams.

Caulfield frowned. To distract him, I looked over at the door. He followed my line of sight, still frowning, wondering where Dehan was. Her voice came from behind him, low and steady and calm. "I think that's exactly what they're going to do, but by the time I've finished with him they may have to tear him a new . . ."

Before she could finish, he was spinning, panicking. He turned to face her with the automatic held out in front of him. In that same moment, I roared and charged at him, headfirst. It wasn't smart, but I wasn't going to let him shoot a woman who looked that good holding an AK-47. In that same moment, the doors burst open behind us and Henry's Alpha Two team came storming in, bellowing and wielding bits of broken wooden pallet over their heads, like a band of raiding Vikings.

My head thundered home into Caulfield's belly just as his automatic barked, and at the same instant, his head rocked as Dehan's shot slammed home right between his eyes.

We crashed to the floor. I heard her scream, "*Stone!*" and I looked up, sick with terror for a moment that she'd been hit. She was rushing at me with fear in her eyes, shouting, "*Are you okay? Are you hit? Did I hit you?*"

I smiled at her. "How many rounds did you fire?"

"One!"

I grinned. "How's Caulfield doing?"

She glanced at him. "Not so good." Then she scowled. "But I was aiming for his arm, you asshole! I had to shift when you charged, you great lummox! I could have killed you!"

I couldn't stop smiling. "Oh . . . It's just, you look so . . ."

The Alpha Two team had put down their wooden swords and were now slowly establishing order. The huge Sergeant Lewis hoisted me to my feet and Henry undid my cuffs. Lewis said, "I heard your little speech, sir. Very inspiring. Thank you."

"Thank *you*, Sergeant."

Dehan held up her cell and handed it to Henry. "You have the whole exchange here."

He smiled and took it. "You are a marvel, Carmen. This silly sod doesn't deserve you."

She winked at me and, ever loyal, she said, "Yeah, he does."

He laughed. "If you say so." Then he was on his radio again, telling Alpha One to set up a perimeter, and calling for a meat wagon, a SOCO team, which is the Brits' version of a crime scene team, and a forensic IT team, because they had found Katie Ellison's laptop, her pen drives, and her notebooks.

The proverbial shit was about to hit the fan, and it was going to be the shitstorm of the century.

EPILOGUE

We were sitting in the VIP lounge at Heathrow Airport, waiting for our flight to be called. We were there courtesy of Lord Chiddester, who had also upgraded our flights, seeing as we had refused to take payment for helping to solve his daughter's murder. Our luggage was all checked in and we had an hour to kill, so we figured we might as well drown it in martinis as shoot it with an AK-47.

Dehan, now dressed in jeans and a demure blouse, was bobbing her olive up and down in her drink, looking pensive.

"It's hard to believe," she said at last, "that something like that could happen in a country like Britain today."

I nodded and ate my olive instead of bobbing it. "The world is changing. I don't know if there ever were certainties. I guess after World War II, everybody thought there were certainties, until Kennedy and Vietnam, and Watergate . . . It was only a very short time when we felt more or less sure about who we were, in the West, and what we were about."

She gave a short laugh that was more like a snort. "I read once that every new century actually starts one or two decades in. You know, the twentieth started in 1916, the eighteenth in 1812. I wonder if we are getting a first taste of what the new century is bringing us."

"That's a kind of scary thought."

She nodded. "On a happier note, Stone, I have decided that in this new and uncertain world, I have acquired a taste for the good life. So we are going to become international consulting detectives to the Crowned Heads of Europe and world governments, uncovering coups and conspiracies and charging exorbitant fees for it."

I frowned at my glass and signaled the barman to refill it. "Stone and Stone, Consulting Detectives, no fee too great, most jobs too small. I like it. However, Dehan, I insist that in all of our investigations, you wear a minute black dress and carry an AK-47."

She shrugged. "I can do that."

We were quiet for a while as the clock hands moved on toward departure time. After a bit, Dehan voiced my own thoughts. "I wonder what's next in the box?"

The box was our collection of cold cases back at the 43rd Precinct.

"I seem to remember it was the Vince Wolowitz case. They found him tied to his bed in his house on St. Lawrence Avenue."

"Oh yeah, Clason Point, near the Catholic church. His dog had got busy on his foot."

"That's the one. Neighbors said he had a hundred grand in a cardboard box under the bed."

"But it was never found."

"What was that, ninety-seven?"

"August ninety-seven. I remember it. You know? I wondered at the time about his family . . ."

"Yeah, I wondered that too . . ."

And the hands of the clock moved on, toward departure.

Don't miss LITTLE DEAD RIDING HOOD. The riveting sequel in the Dead Cold Mystery series.

Scan the QR code below to purchase LITTLE DEAD RIDING HOOD.

Or go to: righthouse.com/little-dead-riding-hood

NOTE: flip to the very end to read an exclusive sneak peak...

DON'T MISS ANYTHING!

If you want to stay up to date on all new releases in this series, with this author, or with any of our new deals, you can do so by joining our newsletters below.

In addition, you will immediately gain access to our entire *Right House VIP Library,* which includes many riveting Mystery and Thriller novels for your enjoyment!

righthouse.com/email

(Easy to unsubscribe. No spam. Ever.)

ALSO BY BLAKE BANNER

Up to date books can be found at:
www.righthouse.com/blake-banner

ROGUE THRILLERS
Gates of Hell (Book 1)
Hell's Fury (Book 2)

ALEX MASON THRILLERS
Odin (Book 1)
Ice Cold Spy (Book 2)
Mason's Law (Book 3)
Assets and Liabilities (Book 4)
Russian Roulette (Book 5)
Executive Order (Book 6)
Dead Man Talking (Book 7)
All The King's Men (Book 8)
Flashpoint (Book 9)
Brotherhood of the Goat (Book 10)
Dead Hot (Book 11)
Blood on Megiddo (Book 12)
Son of Hell (Book 13)

HARRY BAUER THRILLER SERIES
Dead of Night (Book 1)
Dying Breath (Book 2)
The Einstaat Brief (Book 3)
Quantum Kill (Book 4)
Immortal Hate (Book 5)
The Silent Blade (Book 6)
LA: Wild Justice (Book 7)

Breath of Hell (Book 8)
Invisible Evil (Book 9)
The Shadow of Ukupacha (Book 10)
Sweet Razor Cut (Book 11)
Blood of the Innocent (Book 12)
Blood on Balthazar (Book 13)
Simple Kill (Book 14)
Riding The Devil (Book 15)
The Unavenged (Book 16)
The Devil's Vengeance (Book 17)
Bloody Retribution (Book 18)
Rogue Kill (Book 19)
Blood for Blood (Book 20)

DEAD COLD MYSTERY SERIES
An Ace and a Pair (Book 1)
Two Bare Arms (Book 2)
Garden of the Damned (Book 3)
Let Us Prey (Book 4)
The Sins of the Father (Book 5)
Strange and Sinister Path (Book 6)
The Heart to Kill (Book 7)
Unnatural Murder (Book 8)
Fire from Heaven (Book 9)
To Kill Upon A Kiss (Book 10)
Murder Most Scottish (Book 11)
The Butcher of Whitechapel (Book 12)
Little Dead Riding Hood (Book 13)
Trick or Treat (Book 14)
Blood Into Wine (Book 15)
Jack In The Box (Book 16)
The Fall Moon (Book 17)
Blood In Babylon (Book 18)
Death In Dexter (Book 19)
Mustang Sally (Book 20)

A Christmas Killing (Book 21)
Mommy's Little Killer (Book 22)
Bleed Out (Book 23)
Dead and Buried (Book 24)
In Hot Blood (Book 25)
Fallen Angels (Book 26)
Knife Edge (Book 27)
Along Came A Spider (Book 28)
Cold Blood (Book 29)
Curtain Call (Book 30)

THE OMEGA SERIES
Dawn of the Hunter (Book 1)
Double Edged Blade (Book 2)
The Storm (Book 3)
The Hand of War (Book 4)
A Harvest of Blood (Book 5)
To Rule in Hell (Book 6)
Kill: One (Book 7)
Powder Burn (Book 8)
Kill: Two (Book 9)
Unleashed (Book 10)
The Omicron Kill (Book 11)
9mm Justice (Book 12)
Kill: Four (Book 13)
Death In Freedom (Book 14)
Endgame (Book 15)

ABOUT US

Right House is an independent publisher created by authors for readers. We specialize in Action, Thriller, Mystery, and Crime novels.

If you enjoyed this novel, then there is a good chance you will like what else we have to offer! Please stay up to date by using any of the links below.

Join our mailing lists to stay up to date -->
righthouse.com/email
Visit our website --> righthouse.com
Contact us --> contact@righthouse.com

facebook.com/righthousebooks
x.com/righthousebooks
instagram.com/righthousebooks

EXCLUSIVE SNEAK PEAK OF...

LITTLE DEAD RIDING HOOD

CHAPTER 1

"Family." He said it as though it was the answer to a particularly complicated equation. Then he smiled, like he expected me to be amazed at that answer, and turned his smile on Dehan, pulling up his bedclothes as he did so. Rain rattled on the windowpane. A dull, wet glow highlighted his left profile, leaving the right side of his face in semidarkness. He didn't want the lights on. His eyes were too sensitive. There was a smell of encroaching death in the room. I had the feeling it was lying patiently in the corners and in the shadows, waiting to creep forward when nobody was looking. It was the reek of flavorless food, musty clothes, and too much disinfectant. I had a strong urge to get up and leave. My attention strayed through the rain-spattered glass to the sodden lawn. A drip from the eaves sounded like an accelerated clock.

Sean Reynolds was talking again. "Everybody thinks family is an Italian thing." He pronounced it "eye-talian." "Like the Italians invented family. 'Family.'" He wheezed a laugh. "You gotta say it like you're Robert De Niro. But I'm Irish. I'm not Italian. We came over two centuries ago. And let me tell you, family is just as important to an Irishman as it is to any Italian."

Dehan was sitting in a sage-green armchair that looked almost black in the failing light. She said, "Mr. Reynolds, we were told that your son, Samuel, had some new evidence for us..."

"Oh, he has, he won't be long. He's only gone down in the truck to the store. There are things I need, you know. He's a good lad. He brought my bed down to the living room, so's I wouldn't have to climb the stairs. I'm practically bedridden. Family, see? He never married, stayed here with me and Hen."

"Hen?"

"Helen. We call her Hen. Always have. She's not..." He screwed up his face, made a gesture with his finger going around in circles at his temple, and mouthed, *not all there...* We've had some family tragedies. If I told you, believe me."

Dehan nodded. "That's the girl who let us in?"

"Hen, yeah."

"And where is she now? Does she know anything about this new evidence...?"

"Up in her room. She stays in her room. She's on medication. She didn't used to take it, but now Samuel makes sure she takes it. He's a good lad. I don't know..." He said this last as though answering an inaudible query, then shook his head slowly on the pillow and repeated, "I don't know..." Then, after a long pause gazing at the rain outside, he added, "What we'd do without him."

I looked at my watch and drew breath to say that maybe we could come back some other time, but his eyes were glazed and his mind was somewhere else. "Since Eileen died," he said, in that way he had of making statements as though they were related to something nobody had said.

Dehan spoke from the shadows of her chair. "Eileen was your wife."

It wasn't a question, and he didn't answer, he just kept staring at the window, with his mouth slightly open and the covers pulled up almost to his chin.

"Giving birth to Celeste," he said.

"So Celeste never knew her mother?"

He gave his head the most imperceptible shake. "The good Lord gave us Celeste and took away her mother, all on the same night, twenty years ago, on November ninth. Samuel was only six years old. Helen was eight, and poor Celeste came into the world without ever knowing her mom. That was a cruel night." His gaze drifted from the window to rest on Dehan's face. His smile made him look somehow older than he was. He couldn't have been more than sixty-five, but lying there, he might have been a hundred. "We pulled together, as family. I think Samuel realized that night that it was up to him and me to pull through. To pull the family through."

A flurry of wind dragged wet leaves across the patch of lawn visible through the glass. The air seemed to groan through the house, and I heard the front door open and close. Big feet tramped past. We sat in silence and listened to a fridge open and close three times, cupboard doors bang, then big feet tramped back and the door to the room opened.

Samuel occupied the whole doorway. The hall behind him was as dark and gloomy as the room in front of him. He narrowed his eyes to observe Dehan, and then me, where I sat at the foot of the old man's bed. He had an angry face, like it had been cast that way, and he'd look mad whatever mood he was in. His narrowed eyes now made him look angrier. His voice was surprisingly quiet.

"I'm sorry I'm late," he said. "I had to get some things."

I stood and showed him my badge. "Mr. Reynolds, I am Detective John Stone. This is Detective Carmen Dehan." She stood also and showed him her badge. "We run the cold-cases unit at the Forty-Third. We got a message that you have some new evidence relating to a cold case."

He didn't look at our badges. He listened to me, and when I had finished, he went over to his father. "How are you doing, Daddy?" he said. "Will I make you your cocoa?"

My voice was a little louder than I had intended. I sighed and said, "Mr. Reynolds, we are very busy and we can't afford to spend the afternoon sitting around waiting for you. If you have something to tell us, then we would appreciate you doing it now."

He stood erect and scowled at me. "He always has his cocoa at this time."

I pulled a card from my wallet and handed it to him. "When you're ready, call me and come down to the station house."

The old man was flapping his hands. "Sit down, sit down. Samuel, you can't keep the police waiting on you, I'll have my cocoa later. Sit down."

Samuel hesitated a moment, then pulled over a straight-backed chair and sat by the window with the cold, silver light on his face. We sat too, and Dehan pulled a notebook from her pocket.

I said, "Samuel, we got your message and came straight over. We haven't looked at the file yet. So if you could fill us in a little, that would help."

He didn't answer straightaway. When he did, he said, "I asked for Lenny. Lenny had the case."

"Lenny Davis?"

He nodded.

"Detective Davis doesn't work cold cases. Like I said, we run the cold-cases unit. This case is two years old now."

Dehan was making notes. "Don't worry, we'll be sure and talk to him to get us up to speed."

His back was very straight, and he had his big hands on his knees. His trousers were a rusty corduroy. His sweater was a darker rust color, like his tightly curled hair. He wet his lips with his tongue. "I went to see Chad."

Dehan sighed. "Who's Chad?"

"Chad Norris was Celeste's boyfriend, kind of. She was seeing him, used to stay over with him. I always thought he was the one who killed her. I didn't like her seeing him. That's where she was going the night she was killed. To see him."

"Celeste," I said, "was your younger sister. She was eighteen at the time, and you didn't approve of her boyfriend, Chad."

He gave a single nod.

"What was it about him, Samuel, that you didn't like?"

"He was one of those, you know, like he thought he was superior. His dad's got lots of money, and he has his own house his dad bought for him, and he's studying law, going to be a big shot lawyer, you know. Like he was too good for us."

Dehan scratched her head and leaned back in her chair, crossing one long leg over the other. "If he was going out with your sister, how could he think he was too good for you?"

There was a resentful glaze to his eyes now, and a slight curl of the lip. "Well, she was getting ideas herself. Maybe she thought she was too good for us too."

"Samuel!" Sean, the old man, had got up on one elbow. The aged weakness had evaporated from his face. In its place, there was a scowl that instantly cowed his son. "Family! That's your sister!"

I studied the old man's face as he sank back into the pillows, and the appearance of sickness seeped back into the folds and creases. I glanced at Samuel. He was rubbing his palm with his thumb. "So what made you think Chad killed your sister?"

He shrugged. "She was going to his house that night. Probably going to stay the night. She did often enough."

I waited, but there was nothing more. "Forgive me for insisting, Samuel, but going to visit somebody isn't normally a motive for murder. There has to be something more."

"Well, it's him. He's a violent sort, aggressive. He used to attack her . . ."

Dehan looked up from her pad. "Physically?"

"No . . . well . . . She said he used to push her if he got mad. He had a temper. He'd pinch her sometimes too. But mostly it was verbal. He used to humiliate her, shout at her. She told me about it and it made her cry. It made me mad. I told her I'd go talk to him, but she said not to. Like she didn't want him to meet us. Like she was ashamed of us."

"So you never met him?"

"Never till now."

"He lives near here?"

It was his father who answered. "Croes Avenue, not more than five or ten minutes' walk down Gleason." And he told us the number.

I said, "So, what happened that night?"

Samuel said to his hand, "I would have thought you'd know that. Lenny would have known. That's why I thought they'd send him."

I smiled as amiably as I could, though he wasn't looking at me, and in that gloom he probably wouldn't have seen me anyway.

"As I said, Samuel, we were only just handed the case, and we haven't had a chance yet to study the file. What happened that night?"

Again it was his father who answered for Samuel. He was smiling and seemed to be talking to Dehan. "She'd never known her mother. She never had a mother figure, to show her the way. She was my good girl though, hey, Samuel? Lovely, sweet-natured child, couldn't do enough to help around the house. Always obedient and polite."

Samuel was nodding, still rubbing the palm of his hand, like he had a stain there he was trying to remove.

The old man frowned. "But as she got older, the lack of maternal guidance began to tell a little. Samuel and I . . ." He looked over at me as though I would be better equipped to understand the next bit. "We weren't best suited, being men, you know? When she became a woman, we didn't really know . . . how to guide her and that."

Samuel finally looked up from his hand at his father. "We did the best we could, Daddy. But . . ." He looked frankly at Dehan. "No offense, but women can be real hard to understand sometimes. Especially at the time of the month. It's like two out of every five weeks, some women go crazy."

Dehan gave a bark of laughter. "You're not kidding. But don't let the thought police hear you say that."

He gave a small frown like he didn't know what she was talking about. "Anyway, by the time Celeste was sixteen, it seemed she was going to be one of those. She started going out a lot with boys, staying out late, drinking. You know the sort of thing."

His dad was scowling at the floor. "She wasn't a whore!" he said suddenly. "She was a good girl. But when she hit her teens, she went a bit wild. Maybe it was her Irish blood. God knows I was no saint at sixteen—nor at twenty-six! It took your blessed mother to make me settle down. Lord! I miss that woman every day of my life! She would have known how to calm Celeste. She would have known how to talk to her, how to make her see sense. God must know in his wisdom why he had to take her from us, but it nearly killed me when he did. And I believe it killed Celeste."

Dehan frowned. "How's that, Mr. Reynolds?"

"If she had still been with us, Celeste would not have been so wild, I'm sure of it. She would not have been out that night, and if she had, she would have been with a nicer type of man."

"So you also believe Chad might have been responsible for her death?"

"If not him, one like him. They're all the same, boozing, taking drugs, having their damned parties."

Dehan spoke suddenly, "Okay, so, let me see if I've got this straight. Sunday, the sixth of November, she goes out, at night, to walk to Chad's house, five or ten minutes down the road?"

Samuel nodded.

"Okay, so where had she been that weekend?"

"She had spent most of Friday and all of Saturday with him, stayed the night, and came back lunchtime on Sunday." He said all this flatly, without looking at us, in a voice made mechanical by shame.

I asked, "How was she when she got in? Was she her normal self? Did she seem preoccupied?"

Neither of them answered.

I said, "Well?"

The old man said, "You have to remember, Detective, that without a mother to intercede, communication wasn't always easy. Me and Samuel, we can talk to each other, we understand each other, but with Celeste, at that time, she could be sullen."

Samuel said, "And I was angry with her for staying out, so we had words in the kitchen. Daddy come in to sort it out, and the two of us wound up shouting at Celeste, and her shouting back . . ."

"Samuel!"

"Well, they have to know, Daddy! That's how it was. It's nobody's fault! But she wound up storming up the stairs to her room, slamming the door, and not coming out."

Dehan said, "Until?"

The old man answered. "I'll never forget it so long as I live. Eight thirty p.m., she come down those stairs, in her torn jeans, big, black boots like a soldier's boots, her hair—she had lovely, wild red hair—her hair all scrunched under a woolen cap, and a dirty, big, red woolen jacket with a hood. You know, I often think what a tragedy, such a beautiful girl—and she was lovely looking, wasn't she, Samuel?—to die looking so bloody awful. I know that sounds like a shallow thing to say, but it's true all the same." His gaze wandered again, out the window. "Such a lovely girl, to die looking like a tramp. When she had her home and her family to care for her."

"So when she came down the stairs, did she say anything?"

Samuel said, "I asked her where she was going, she gave me a mouthful of abuse and said she was going to see Chad. She said at least she felt welcome there."

"And she left?"

"Maybe more things were said. I went to the kitchen. Daddy was begging her to see sense. She walked out and slammed the door behind her."

His daddy had started to sob. He had a big, boney hand over his face and he was making ugly, visceral noises.

Samuel said, "He has angina and high blood pressure. This isn't good for him."

The old man uncovered his face and reached out to us with his other hand. His face was wet and twisted with grief. "I don't want you to go! I want to help! I want to hear what you talk about. It's been two years waiting and I swear it's killing me. I need to hear what you say and what you think... Don't go."

I studied him a moment. "We won't keep you much longer, Mr. Reynolds. Just a couple more questions. After Celeste left that night, none of you heard from her again?"

He started sobbing again and Samuel said, "No. Not till the police—well, Lenny—told us she'd been found, down by the river."

I looked at Samuel. "You said you had new evidence, Samuel."

His expression didn't change, but he drew himself up, and there was a challenge in his eyes. "I got tired of waiting for nothing to happen, and I went and talked to Chad."

"When was this?"

"This morning. I told him I thought he'd killed Celeste. He said I was crazy and I ought to be careful making that kind of accusation. Threatened me with all his lawyer talk. I told him I wasn't scared and maybe we should have the whole thing aired in court. He said I was probably stupid enough to do that, and I said that maybe I was. That was when he told me."

"Told you what, Samuel?"

"That she was seeing other men. He said they were both getting tired of each other. He was finding her boring, he said. That they were never serious about having a future together, and that she was seeing at least one other man."

"How did he know that?"

"He said he caught her sending text messages to some guy."

"Did he know these men?"

He shook his head. "He said he didn't. But I reckon he killed her 'cause he was jealous, and now he's just covering up, pretending he don't care. I'll tell you something, he has a wild temper. He can get real mad."

I sighed and glanced at Dehan. She gave me a nod. I said, "Okay, I think what we need to do now is go and study the file, and we may need to get back to you again after that. Do you still have Celeste's things?"

Her father said, "Her room is just as it was the day she left. We haven't had the heart to do anything with it."

"We may need to go through her things at some point, so if you can just keep that room locked for now." I looked at Dehan and we both stood.

The old man said, "You should talk to Lenny. He knows all about it."

"You and Lenny friends?"

He nodded. "Sure. We go back a long way. We grew up in the same street. I was older than him, taught him his way around." He laughed. "Ask him. He'll tell you. 'You know old Sean Reynolds?' He'll know."

I smiled. "I'll be sure to talk to him."

Samuel let us out onto Beach Avenue and closed the door behind us. I noticed a cream Toyota pickup truck parked outside the gate. The rain had stopped, but odd, icy drops were still falling from fat, low-slung gray clouds, propelled by sporadic gusts of wind. We walked in silence toward my old, burgundy Jaguar. Rusty, wet leaves had gathered in drifts around its spoked wheels and, though it was only five in the afternoon, the lights were coming on in the windows down the street, and headlamps were reflecting wet across the blacktop.

As Dehan stood by the passenger door, she asked me, "You want to grab some coffee and pull the file?"

I nodded like I was agreeing, because my mind was on something else. Then I shook it and said, "No, I already pulled the file. It's on the back seat. I want to take a five- or ten-minute walk down Gleason Avenue and have a chat with Chad. I think we should see just how formidable his temper really is."

CHAPTER 2

We walked among the eclectic jumble of clapboard and red brick that is Gleason Avenue, with the cold, desultory breeze creeping around our ankles and feeling its way into gaps and openings in our coats and sleeves. Heavy traffic, homeward bound, hissed over wet asphalt, or waited rumbling in long lines at the traffic lights, which gleamed off shiny, wet chassis and lay like spilled, luminous liquid among the puddles.

We went three blocks and came to the Watson Gleason Playground, skirted on all four sides by giant chestnut trees. Opposite the entrance to the playground, there was a large, redbrick building. On the corner there was a grocery store, and above it apartments. I pointed at the windows and said, "The only witness Lenny could find lived in that apartment up there."

Dehan looked surprised. "How do you know?"

"When I pulled the file, I had a quick read."

"Why didn't you tell me?"

"You were getting coffee. I didn't want to distract you."

"Jerk."

We dodged through the traffic and I rang on the bell beside a bright, red door. Dehan was still making a question at me with her face. I smiled. "You were talking to the inspector. I found the file, leafed through it, and had a quick look, happened to notice there was only one witness. Don't get touchy."

"Don't cut me out." She poked me on the chest. "You know it makes me mad."

The door opened to reveal a plump woman in her late twenties or early thirties. She had thick, black hair in a big halo around her head and huge brown eyes that were itching to laugh. She seemed to be dressed in amorphous brown cloth bags and leaned on the doorjamb chewing gum.

"You cops? I was just going to the store." She made it sound like "sto-wa."

I smiled back at her eyes and that made her grin. "We won't keep you. Are you Remedios Borja?"

"Not if you're gonna arrest me."

"We're not."

"Then that's me. You got me." She laughed as though she'd made a joke.

Dehan made a strange face that should have been a smile but wasn't and said, "Do you remember a couple of years back, you made a statement to the police? It was a murder investigation?"

"Uh-huh. But I don't remember much. It's rained a lot since then, right?"

I gave her a warm smile, which made her grin again. "Just tell us what you saw."

She shrugged. "Not a lot." She pointed across the road. "It was like nine o'clock, maybe a bit earlier. It was dark. I'd left the drapes open. It was around this time of year, November. It was cold. I dunno, I guess I'd been in the kitchen, whatever, I left the drapes open. So I went to close them. And when I did, I saw this girl just, like, standing, right over there on the corner, near the tree."

She pointed at the giant chestnut outside the gate to the playground. We both turned to look. I said, "She was just standing there?"

"Uh-huh. I thought at first she was a whore, and that made

me mad 'cause we don't get whores around here. This is a nice neighborhood. But then I thought she didn't really look like a hooker. Her clothes, her hair. She looked a mess."

"Can you remember how she was dressed?"

"Oh sure. I wouldn't forget that. It wasn't raining, but it was kind of drizzling? And she had on this big-ass old red jacket. I think it was a couple of sizes too big for her, with the hood over her head. And she was standing, with her hands in her pockets . . ."

I asked, "Which way was she facing, Remedios?"

"Oh, she was facing down toward White Plains . . ."

"East."

She grinned. "If you say so. Anyhow, next thing I see, there's a guy there, and they are talkin' and he seems to be mad. She looks pretty mad too."

Dehan said, "Can you describe him?"

"He was tall, taller than her, anyhow. Big. He had a leather jacket, I think, and one of them woolen hats that roll down? Can't say more than that."

I said, "What happened next?"

"Next thing, she's shouting at him. We got triple glazing, so I couldn't hear what she was saying. But he grabs her shoulders and starts kind'a shaking her. She slaps him and she turns and disappears behind that big tree there . . ." She pointed at the second giant chestnut. "After that, I lost sight of them and closed the drapes."

I frowned. "Did you see if he went after her?"

"Oh, for sure. He definitely went after her. He was kind of half running and reaching out for her."

Dehan shook her head. "You didn't think to call the cops?"

Remedios rolled her eyes. "Don't give me no lecture, sister. If I called the cops every time I see a boy put his hand on a girl, or a girl give a boy some attitude, this place would be crawlin' with cops twenty-four fockin' seven. I called the cops when I read about the girl in the river, with the big red coat. You feel me?"

I said, "Yeah, we feel you. Did anybody else see anything?"

"Nobody talked to me about it."

"Okay, thanks, Remedios. You've been very helpful."

"Sure, anytime."

She watched us cross the road through the traffic again and continue west toward Croes Avenue.

Dehan fell into step beside me, watching her boots as she trod the wet sidewalk. She spoke to no one in particular, simply voicing her thoughts.

"So she spends most of Friday and Saturday with Chad. The whole day and the night. She comes home Sunday midday. She and Samuel get into a big row in the kitchen and Dad comes in to break it up, but winds up joining Samuel in giving Celeste a piece of his mind." She looked up at me. "Have you noticed how Samuel calls his dad Daddy? Is that weird?"

I nodded, but I didn't say anything.

She added, "Especially when they talk so much about family. It's like he never grew up and became a man. Am I being judgmental?"

"Probably, but I know what you mean. Keep going, she gets mad and storms upstairs," I said. "We don't know what she does up there, but she doesn't come down for a few hours."

"Sometime between half past eight and nine o'clock. One thing stands out a mile. She was sick of her father and Samuel, and Samuel had had about a bellyful of her. And I think that goes for her dad too. He makes a big show of not criticizing her, but privately, I am pretty sure he and Samuel had both had about as much of her as they could swallow."

I looked at her curiously. "Are you suggesting Samuel killed his sister?"

She stuck out her bottom lip and shoved her hands in her back pockets, then looked up into my face. "No . . . not necessarily. But I sure as hell wouldn't rule him out." She shrugged. "Five, ten minutes after she walked out of the house, she stops at the playground to wait for somebody. A guy who could fit Samuel's description turns up and they have a row. She tries to walk away, and he goes after her. Next time anybody sees Celeste, she's dead, washed up on the banks of the Bronx River. And . . ." She half turned back the way we'd come. "She was waiting, looking back the way she'd come."

"So you think, what? That Samuel phoned her, told her to wait for him, and came after her to continue their row?"

"It's not an impossible scenario."

"No, it's not impossible, but is it likely she would stand waiting for him to continue a row she has just walked out on twice before?"

She grunted.

I pointed up ahead. We were approaching a twenty-story tower block on the right. "This is it, here on the left."

Chad's house was an ugly, flat, redbrick construction with four sash windows on the upper floor and four concrete steps behind an iron railing and gate leading up to a white front door.

Dehan went in ahead of me and rang the bell, but by that time we could already hear the shouting inside. She had to ring three times and eventually hammer on the wood before thumping feet approached and the door was wrenched open. The guy who wrenched it open was probably twenty-five with expensively cut blond hair, pale blue eyes, and a face that was cruelly handsome. He was slim, in Levi's jeans and a Columbia University sweatshirt. His eyes flicked over Dehan, then over me, and he said, "What?"

She showed him her badge and I showed him mine.

"I'm Detective Carmen Dehan. This is my partner, Detective John Stone. Are you Chad Norris?"

"Yeah. Why?"

"We'd like to talk to you about Celeste Reynolds."

He gave a small sigh through his nose. He gazed at the wall, chewing his lip, then he stared at the corner of the door. He put his hands on his hips and stepped away from us, then turned back. "You know, I'm just wondering," he said, "what could you do—no, seriously—what could you do to make my day any *fucking worse*? No, I mean it, go ahead, do it! I mean, my roommate just broke my *damned television*! I tell him to leave *and he starts crying like a fucking girl*!" He stared up the stairs, as though he wanted to see if his roommate could hear him. "*Can you hear me? You fucking pussy!*"

I said, "Mr. Norris, unfortunately, we haven't got time to wait for you to grow up. If you can't talk to us now, then perhaps you could come down to the station, but one way or another, we need to talk to you."

He came down the stairs again and walked toward us, jerking out his knees and blinking. "I'm sorry. You haven't got time for *what*?"

I watched him with interest.

He said again, "You haven't got time for *what*?"

Dehan looked up at me. "Would you say his manner was threatening, Stone? He looks out of control to me." Before I could answer, she had turned back to him. "Sir, have you been consuming drugs or alcohol? Have you got drugs or alcohol on the premises? You seem to me to be out of control and somewhat threatening in your manner."

Suddenly, Chad Norris was smiling. His hands were up and he was laughing. "Whoa, whoa, whoa! Take it easy there, tiger! Okay, okay, why don't we start again without the attitude. I was mad. I apologize. I was certainly *not* threatening you in any way!" With a touch of sarcasm, he gestured us inside with both hands, like a waiter guiding us to a table. "How about you come in, and, please, tell me how I can help you?"

I gave him a humorless smile. "Yeah, how about that?"

The house looked newly decorated. A broad, light hallway with polished wooden floors was laid with a cream carpet that climbed a staircase to the upper floor. The banisters and the walls were also painted cream, and on the left a bare pine door stood open onto a room with white calico sofas and armchairs. Chad made for the stairs with an unpleasant smile on his face.

"Go right on in. I'll be with you in a moment. I just need to deal with something upstairs."

The room was dominated by a vast, black, flat-screen TV on a stand. Aside from the sofa and the chair, there was practically no furniture, except for a coffee table piled with magazines and books on law. French doors stood closed, spattered with rain in the failing light, offering a view of an unkempt backyard with an overgrown lawn. Pretty soon, we heard Chad's voice hollering upstairs:

"*You get the fuck out of my house! I don't give a damn what you do. Just get out! You have fifteen minutes to get your shit together and get out!*"

A door slammed and feet thumped down the stairs. Chad entered the room and stopped, smiling at us both in turn. "Sometimes you just have to tell it how it is. Then you feel better." He gestured at the sofa with both hands. "Sit."

He sat. Dehan sat in the corner of the sofa. I remained standing by the French doors.

"You want to talk to me about Celeste."

Dehan answered, "We're from the cold-cases unit at the Forty-Third."

"You guys have one of those? I thought that was just on TV." His smile was amiable, but there was no hiding the sarcasm in his eyes. Dehan carried on as though he hadn't spoken.

"We're reviewing Celeste's case, and we understand that you two were pretty close."

He nodded at her, still smiling amiably. "What of it?"

Dehan raised an eyebrow. "That's it? 'What of it?' That's your reply?"

He gave a small laugh. "Forgive me, perhaps it's all the browbeating we get at Columbia: 'Be precise! Be precise! What, exactly, are you saying?' But I am not clear exactly what you are asking me. You are correct. Celeste and I were, at one time, close."

Dehan sat forward with her elbows on her knees and took a

moment to study the backs of her fingers. "I hadn't got around to asking you any questions yet, Chad, but when I do, I promise you they will be very precise." Now she raised her eyes to meet his. "Working on the assumption that you want us to find your girlfriend's killer, I was inviting you to engage with us and share information."

"Oh, well, now, see, she wasn't exactly my girlfriend. We were more like friends with benefits."

"Not much of a benefit to her."

He shrugged and spread his hands. "What do you want me to say? Her getting killed had nothing to do with being my friend."

"Well that's not exactly true, is it, Chad?" She was studying the backs of her long fingers again. "Because she was on her way to see you when she disappeared."

He gave his head a quick shake. "Oh, but you don't know that for a fact, do you?"

I laughed. "What's that thing you guys are so fond of quoting? 'The truth is a philosophical concept. Fact is something you can prove in court.' Well, we know for a fact that she was on her way to see you when she was last seen alive. Now, we have a lot of very precise questions that we would like to ask about that. Like, did she ever get here? What happened when she did? But right now what we would prefer, Chad, is for you to drop the Ivy League attorney act and make like you give a damn that she was killed. Tell us about that weekend."

He gaped at me for a while, then blinked and readjusted his ass on the chair. "Well, *of course* I give a damn. But, you know, it was two years ago. You have to move on, right? But I was really cut up about her death. Ask any one of my friends!"

Dehan smiled sweetly at him. "You have any left from back then?"

He swallowed. His face said he was wondering if he had.

I said, "Just tell us about that weekend, Chad. Try to stick to the truth. I mean the philosophical concept. It has a way of coming out and biting you in the ass if you ignore it."

I moved and sat on the sofa, and he started to talk.

CHAPTER 3

"You have to understand that one thing I do not have is time. Law at Columbia is a total commitment. And the people who do not commit fail. It is that simple. Commitment is the baseline, it's what you do on top of commitment that makes you a winner. And what you do on top is sacrifice things that other people take for granted as a normal part of life: parties, girlfriends, evenings in front of the TV, chilling, eating pizza . . . All that will come, and more. But right now—and back then—it is focus, focus, focus. My dad summed it up for me when I was a kid, and I always remember what he said. 'Focus is commitment, and commitment is focus.'

"So there is only one way you can have a girlfriend in a situation like this. It's like the Clintons. She wasn't just helping him and supporting him, she was there doing it with him. But how many women are there with the focus and drive of Hillary? Right?"

The question was directed at me, but then he looked at Dehan and said, "No offense."

"None taken. Believe me."

"So I have no time for a romantic attachment. I have needs, like all guys, but I can't commit to a woman. So along comes

Celeste. I can't even remember where we met. It was at a club. One of the rare occasions when I went out. She was there and hunting for a guy, and a mutual acquaintance introduced us."

Dehan was shaking her head. "Wait a minute. Hunting for a guy? What does that mean?"

He shrugged and made a face. "You know! Girls like Celeste, they have no money, but they want a good time, so they hang around clubs where guys with money go and they hunt. Sometimes they hunt in packs, sometimes they go solo. They find a guy who looks like he has money and they close in. Maybe it's a one-night stand, maybe it develops into a long-term solution for their lives.

"So she was cute, she was kind of wild, we had fun, and I told her, in the morning, I don't do this. I am not a party guy. I am focused on my career and nothing is going to get in the way of that." He laughed. "Well, it had the opposite effect from what I had intended. It was like music to her ears, man. I kept telling her, look, we are just friends with benefits. I am not going to marry you. When I marry, it will be the daughter of some CEO, and there will be a prenup that ensures if we ever divorce, I will come out of it a rich man. Sorry!" He hunched his shoulders in a way that said he really wasn't. "You wanted truth. That's truth. I think at first she didn't believe it, but after a bit, things were not so good between us . . ."

Dehan asked, "What does that mean?"

"She was becoming a bit suffocating." He appealed to me. "You know how chicks can get. She was, like, always around. I was like, 'Don't you have a fucking home to go to?' I mean . . ." He flopped back in the chair and sighed. "I didn't want to kick her out because of the sex, right? But it was becoming a case of diminishing returns. You know? She was becoming boring, and the sex just wasn't so good anymore. So, things were getting a little tense."

I asked, "Were you having rows?"

He shook his head. "Celeste didn't row. If you got mad at

Celeste, she just screamed at you a couple of times and walked away."

"Where'd she go?"

He shrugged and made a face of absolute ignorance. "I have no idea, man. She would just leave the house, but before long, she'd be right back again."

Dehan said, "So what happened that weekend?"

He sat forward, elbows on knees, rubbed his face, and sighed. "She came over in the morning on Friday and stayed the night. You have to understand, Saturday to me is just like any other day. I can't go to the examining board and say, 'Hey, my examination is not up to scratch because I spent the damned weekend with a chick who wanted me to pay attention to her.' 'Oh, okay, Mr. Norris, don't worry, we'll give you an A anyway!' It doesn't happen that way."

"So what happened?"

"I went upstairs to get away from her and Nigel . . ." He froze. His face flushed with anger. "Did he leave yet? Did you hear him leave?"

I raised an eyebrow at him. "Stay focused, Chad. What happened?"

He took a deep breath and bit his lip. "Okay! So I went upstairs to get away from Celeste and Nigel, in my own house, I went upstairs to get away from their *incessant yammering*! And the damned TV! I guess she spent the day here and in the evening I came down, they had opened a bottle of wine, and I had a glass. She goes up to the john and while she's up there, Nigel starts telling me I should know when I am onto a good thing. I am not likely to find a girl as good and loyal as Celeste. She really loves me, I should take more care of her, yadda yadda yadda. Bottom line, if I am not careful, she will find somebody else."

"Was he saying that he was interested in her?"

He burst out laughing. "Nigel? Nah! Nigel is gay. He likes sailors with striped shirts and big moustaches. *Isn't that right, Nigel?*" There was a little gasp from the door, the stamping of feet, and the front door slammed. "Son of a bitch was at the door all along."

I sighed. "So what did he mean, she would find somebody else?"

He nodded several times. "I know, right? She's eating here, she's sleeping here, she's watching my TV, using my utilities, and all the while she's fucking some other guy. So I took her phone and I started looking through the messages. And I see there is this guy..." He thought for a moment. "Rod? Rod, yeah, and he is sending her all these messages about how hot she is and how he wants to do this to her and that to her..."

Dehan said, "And how was she responding to these messages?"

He stared hard at her, with eyes that were almost calculating. "That was the smart thing, right? She didn't respond in kind. Her replies were all short. But, each one of them had *something* to encourage him. She was enticing him to believe that there could be something between them, if..."

"If what?"

"I told you at the start. Chicks like Celeste are predators. They're out hunting for a guy who will solve their problems. If she was going to sleep with him, she wanted something in return. She wasn't a hooker, but she was a whore."

"Did you confront her with the messages?"

"You bet your sweet ass I did!"

She stared at him for a long moment. "Watch your mouth there, Chad. What happened when you told her you'd looked at her phone?"

"At first, she was mad and started screaming at me that I had no right to check her phone. But then when I started reading the stuff this guy had written to her, she started crying and apologizing. I asked her how many other guys she was screwing around with. She said she wasn't screwing around with anybody. It was just this guy, it was a game, she was going to tell him to get lost.."

I scratched my head. "Chad. You need to explain this to me. You say she was not your girlfriend. You were just friends with benefits. Yet you got mad when you discovered she'd been cheating on you. You have a big bust-up and I'm guessing you kicked her out..."

He gave a small laugh and looked down at the carpet. "Not exactly."

"Not exactly? What does that mean?"

He shrugged. "The bust-up was kind of hot, and you know... Makeup sex is the best. She spent the night again, we chilled in the morning, and then she went home around midday."

I scratched my Adam's apple for a bit, trying to visualize the scene. It wasn't all that hard. "Did she contact you again during the afternoon?"

"Yeah, she sent me a couple of messages." He shrugged. "You know, the usual stuff, she loved me, that kind of shit."

Dehan said, "What about Rod?"

He shrugged. "What about him?"

"Did she say she was going to dump him? How did you leave that? You were pretty mad at her because of him."

He stared at a couple of walls for a bit, like he was embarrassed. "Yeah, she said she was going to tell him to lay off. She wasn't into him anyway. She'd been kind of stringing him along for a laugh."

"So do you know him? Do you know who he is?"

He shook his head. "Nah, she said he was some guy she knew. I never met him. Anyway, she said she was going to tell him to leave her alone."

I narrowed my eyes and shook my head. "It never occurred to you that this guy might have been the one who killed her?"

His face went a pasty, yellow color. "No..."

Dehan stared at me. "Can you believe this guy? Ivy League." She looked back at him. "You seriously expect me to believe that you saw those sexually explicit messages, you saw that she was teasing him and giving him the come-on, and *the night after* you force her to break it off, she disappears, and you didn't connect the dots? You did not see that there was a possible, *probable*, connection between her disappearance and breaking off with this guy!"

He shook his head. "No . . . She stopped coming around. I thought maybe, even though we'd had the makeup, she'd had enough. Maybe it was just over and that was like the grand finale. Plus, I thought maybe she'd hooked up with this guy after all. That can happen. You meet to break up and you end up getting together. I didn't find out she'd been killed for a few weeks. By that time, I'd moved on, man. I didn't really think about it."

"You're a piece of work, Chad. You're a real piece of work. So did she tell you she was coming over Sunday night or not?"

He shook his head. "No, she just sent me a couple of messages in the afternoon saying she loved me. And that was the last I heard from her."

I asked, "Did you answer those messages?"

"Yeah." He looked embarrassed again. "I told her I loved her too."

Dehan gave him a look that might have withered a sequoia. "Don't worry, your secret is safe with us. Nobody will ever know you pretended to be a human being once."

She made a question with her face and showed it to me. Had I any more questions? I shook my head and stood.

"Your father was right, Chad. Focus and commitment are two sides of the same coin. But they aren't the answer to life's problems. The real secret is knowing what to focus on. If you focus on being a cheap shit all your life, then cheap shit is what life is going to give you. Enjoy your evening."

Scan the QR code below to purchase LITTLE DEAD RIDING HOOD.
Or go to: righthouse.com/little-dead-riding-hood

Made in United States
Troutdale, OR
06/27/2025